Blood
on the
Mountain

A Western Frontier Adventure

Book 1 of the Moses Calhoun
Mountain Westerns

◇

Robert Peecher

For information the author may be contacted at

PO Box 967; Watkinsville GA; 30677

or at mooncalfpress.com

This is a work of fiction. Any similarities to actual events in whole or in part are purely accidental. None of the characters or events depicted in this novel are intended to represent actual people.

FOR JEAN

PEECHER

- 1 -

Old Eli Simmons heard the crunch of the frost on the ground.

He did not think it would be an Indian. In his experience, the Indians didn't make so much noise like a jackass coming through the woods at dusk.

All the same, Old Eli dropped a hand to the leather scabbard that held his fighting knife, a heavy, straight-bladed Arkansas Toothpick. It served as his fighting knife, but also his biscuit-buttering knife, his steak cutting knife, and his whittling knife. It was not, though, his skinning knife. Old Eli carried a curve-bladed knife that he used for skinning, the only use he put that knife to.

The fire was a mite big, and Old Eli now acknowledged to himself that he'd made a mistake to build it up so big. He'd trusted to the fog to keep anyone from seeing the smoke, but the wet air had a way of holding the scent among the tree tops.

Eli Simmons cast his eyes in the direction of the crunching frost, but through the grayness of the trees and the grayness of the fog and the grayness of the dusk, he could not see anyone approaching.

It might be a cat, Eli thought. Not a bear. Bear sounded different, heavier. But it wasn't likely a cat, neither. In the many years he'd lived in these mountains, he heard all sorts of animals make noises. There was a time, a long time ago, when he could not distinguish a squirrel from a cat nor a goat from a bear. But he was better now at identifying the noises animals made, especially when they were trying to make no noise, and Old Eli Simmons was fairly certain the animal trying to sneak up on him now was of the two-legged variety.

But not an Indian.

"I'd have had you if I'd wanted," a familiar voice said. "A man could smell that fire in Kentuck."

Eli Simmons chuckled and set his scabbard back on a rock beside his fire.

"You could have had no such thing," Eli Simmons said, still uncertain exactly where his visitor was. "I heard you coming up when you was clear down at the stream below."

A scoffing laugh, and then a man dressed in skins with a heavy bearskin coat stepped out of the grayness of the forest and into the little clearing where Eli Simmons had made his camp.

"You might have heard me coming from the stream below, but I come from up above," the man said with a grin. He stood still at the edge of the campsite, a polite distance away from Eli Simmons. "Mind if I warm my toes?"

"Suit yourself," the old man said. "And you're welcome, Mose."

The man carried in his folded arms a long Poor-Boy rifle, modeled after the Lancaster rifles of Pennsylvania, but without fancy adornments. The sights and the lock and the rest of the furniture on the gun was all made of iron, not steel, and there were no brass pieces to make it shine. Moses Calhoun called his flintlock gun a "Tennessee rifle." But most folks called it a "Poor-Boy."

The rifle marked Moses Calhoun as an independent man. The men who carried the Lancasters, with their brass and steel to pretty them up, were men who at one time or another had been in the employ of one of the big outfits back East that paid wages for skins and hides.

But a man who carried a Poor-Boy told the world that he'd come up into these mountains on his own and he'd stayed that way. Whatever he hunted or trapped was his own, and he did not owe any piece of it to another man.

Moses Calhoun sat on the ground and leaned his rifle against a tree. Over one shoulder he had a possibles bag, and he pulled that off and set it on one side of him. Over the other shoulder he carried a canteen. He took that off over his head and popped the cork to get a drink. Then he set the canteen down beside him. He worked to pull off his deerskin boots. Eli Simmons watched him with interest. It had been some time since the two men had seen each other.

Calhoun slid off the wool socks, exposing feet that showed the signs of heavy usage.

"About froze," Moses Calhoun said with an apologetic grin.

He laid out the wool socks on a couple of the rocks ringing Eli's fire and set his boots on the rocks beside them.

Calhoun then leaned back on his elbows and set his heels onto the boots so that they would not be directly on the rocks, and he wiggled his toes as the heat from the fire started to thaw them out.

"There is not much worse than cold toes," Calhoun said, tilting his own a bit closer to the flames.

Calhoun looked into the tops of the trees and squinted, as if trying to recall some distant memory.

"I'm trying to bring to mind a time when I've seen you build such a large fire as this one," Moses Calhoun said, and then he turned his squint on Eli Simmons.

The old man grinned.

"I've found as I get older that the bones catch a chill easier than they once did," Eli Simmons said. "I'm like a woman now in the way I prefer my comforts."

Moses Calhoun laughed appreciatively. In the mountains where a man might go weeks without hearing anything more than the wind in the trees or the babble of a stream, humor came in small enough doses.

"Fire large as this one could draw attention," Moses Calhoun said.

Old Eli Simmons tilted his head and looked at the fire.

"It's not so large," he said.

"It puts off enough smoke, anyway," Moses Calhoun said. "I smelled it from up yonder."

"And you thought to come pay a visit to your neighbor?" the old man asked.

Eli Simmons' beard had turned whiter than the last time the two men had been together. It was long and full, and Eli had pulled it tight just below his chin and tied a leather strap around it to keep it from getting in his way.

He wore a beaver skin hat, lined with fur on the inside, and flaps fell over his ears that were tied under his chin. Like Moses, he wore a heavy coat made of bearskin.

"You look warm," Moses Calhoun said. "No holes in your boots?"

"None," Eli said proudly. "Water-tight."

"Mine, too," Moses Calhoun said. "But the level of the stream tested the height of my boots, and found them to be insufficient."

Eli Simmons chuckled.

"I thought you said you come from up above."

Moses Calhoun nodded.

"I crossed the stream a while back and then made my climb. I've been treading in water ever since."

Old Eli nodded, and both men fell silent. They'd shared already more conversation than either man was accustomed to, and it didn't seem to either one that anything more needed to be said right away.

Moses Calhoun enjoyed the warmth he felt against the bottoms of his feet, but he knew he flesh would be cooked before the wool socks and boots were fully dried.

After some time, Calhoun leaned forward, keeping his heels on his boots so that he had tightened himself into an awkward ball, and he flipped his socks over and scooted them a bit closer to the fire. He then took a couple of sticks Eli Simmons had collected earlier and put them into the fire.

"For a man who doesn't like big fires, you certainly seem to be enjoying this one," Old Eli noted.

Calhoun grunted.

"It's not the fire I object to. It's those things the fire might attract."

Eli chuckled.

"Well, if that ain't something to say," Eli Simmons laughed. "You're all I've seen attracted to this fire."

"I suppose I may be at that," Moses Calhoun said.

"Have you et supper yet today?"

Moses shook his head.

"I have not."

Eli picked up the bone-handle of his fighting knife and slid the knife from his scabbard. He stood up and looked around, and finally walked over to a small pine sapling. He quickly stripped two thin branches bare and sharpened one end of each into a point.

He returned to his seat beside the fire, and that was the first that Moses Calhoun saw that Eli had found a large flat stone to use as a chair. There was a time when Eli Simmons wouldn't have turned up his nose over sitting in the dirt.

Old Eli reached into his leather satchel and took out something wrapped in cloth. He laid that open to reveal a side of bacon, and he began cutting away thick strips of it. He speared the strips and leaned forward to hand one of the sticks with the speared bacon to Moses Calhoun.

"Obliged to you," Moses said, taking the stick. He held the bacon over the fire. Eli took up the other stick and did likewise.

Silence returned now as the two men cooked the bacon over the open flames. Grease dropped down off the bacon and sizzled in the flames.

"What brings you so far up this late in the year?" Moses Calhoun asked.

"Huh? Am I so far up?"

"I heard you'd taken a cabin in a town down below."

Old Eli Simmons dropped his eyes.

"You've heard right," he confessed. "I give up last year. Took up town life. I have a chimney now, and I build my fires as large as I like without concern for what might or mightn't attract to it."

Moses Calhoun touched the bacon with his free hand. It was hot and he pulled his hand back quickly, then put his finger and thumb in his mouth. He tasted the bacon grease on his fingertips and decided he would suffer the burns for a bite. He leaned the stick against his leg and used both hands to break off some of the bacon, and he quickly tossed it into his mouth. Steam rose up in front of his face.

"My, that's tasty," he said.

Eli Simmons followed a similar pattern to get at a bite of his bacon.

"What brings you out on a cold night?" Eli Simmons asked.

"Bah. It's not so cold. But I'm trying to get home before dark," Moses said.

"Eh? Is that right? What kind of home have you got?"

"A cabin on a ridge about six miles from here," Moses said.

Eli Simmons narrowed his eyes.

"A cabin six miles from here, and we're sitting on frozen ground eating bacon off a stick?"

"Well, you offered, and I did not want to be impolite," Moses Calhoun said.

"Are you going to invite me to stay the night in your cabin?"

"I thought I would," Moses said.

"We won't make six miles before dark overtakes us," Eli said.

"I know the way," Moses told him. "Let's not let this bacon go to waste, and when we've finished it, we'll cut a trail."

Both men ate, but only a slice of bacon a piece – even thick bacon – did not take long to finish. When it was gone, Moses Calhoun slid his socks back on. He could not tell if they were still a little wet, but they were unquestionably warmer. Then he tugged at his boots, first one and then the other, until they were also back on. While he resumed his footwear, Old Eli Simmons stood up and began kicking dirt over his fire and kicking the coals down.

"How have you come so far without a mule?" Moses asked.

"Two days ago a grizz took my mule," he said. "It was the mule or me, so I let him have the mule. Lost most of my supplies, too."

The man collected his rifle, a Lancaster, and his own possibles bag.

"No water?" Moses Calhoun asked, looking at him.

"Been making do with stream water," Eli said. "The mule had possession of my canteen when the bear took possession of him.."

Calhoun looked around. The gray was turning black. Night would be upon them very soon.

"Stay close," he said.

"Don't worry about me," Eli Simmons said. "I'll not miss the promise of not sleeping in the rain tonight."

Eli Simmons stomped down the coals one last time, and Moses Calhoun poured a little water from his canteen on a particular spot that was still orange with hot coals. He then handed the canteen to the old man, who took a grateful drink.

The two men then started up the slope, making their way to a ridge higher up. Eli Simmons breathed hard as he climbed. Hearing him, Moses Calhoun slowed down some, turning often to lend a hand on particularly large steps or steep spots. Though it pained him to accept the help, Eli Simmons always took the offered hand.

Darkness fell long before they neared the cabin, and with it came a bitter chill. But the two men trudged on. When they'd topped the ridge and the trail had been on an easier grade for some time, Moses heard that the old man breathing easier.

"You didn't say what brought you up so late in the year," Moses reminded him.

"That's right," Eli said. "I failed to answer you."

They continued to walk along in the dark, Moses finding his way by memory. For a time he thought the old man would not give him an answer, but then he began to speak.

"The soldiers are making a winter campaign," he said. "Before I left the town they come in and made camp and started to provision. They were looking for a local man to serve as a guide. They come to me, but I turned 'em down."

Moses turned his head to look at the old man, but it was too dark to see his features.

"Making a campaign against whom?" Moses Calhoun asked.

"The Snake people wintering in the valley yonder," Eli Simmons said.

Moses Calhoun gave some thought to this.

"The soldiers don't make campaigns this time of year," Calhoun said.

Eli Simmons grunted a dismissive response.

"They're making an exception," Eli said. "The white folks are all riled up over some killings."

"Hmm," Moses Calhoun said. "Killings are likely to rile people."

The two men walked on for a while, and though he could not see it, Eli Simmons became aware that they were now making their way down a long draw.

"Is this cabin of yourn much farther?" he asked.

"We're more than half the way," Moses said. "At the bottom of this draw we'll climb a little ways and then come to a high ridge. The cabin is there."

Eli was breathing hard again, even though the terrain was not so difficult.

"If we're more than half the way, this might be a spot where an old man can rest and catch his breath," Eli

14

suggested.

And so they did.

"What have the soldiers and their campaign to do with you?" Moses Calhoun asked when Eli had had a drink of water and caught his breath.

"I fear a massacre is coming," Eli Simmons said. "They have warrants for two chiefs, claiming they are responsible for various attacks on farmers and travelers. But they're coming so late in the year, and when they find them Injuns named on them warrants, they'll find them at their winter camp."

"Women and children," Moses Calhoun said.

"My daughter among 'em," Eli said.

Calhoun cocked his head in surprise.

Moses Calhoun had known Eli Simmons some years now. The two men had hunted and trapped together many times. Eli was not so old when Moses Calhoun first came into the mountains to hunt and trap, and in those days, Eli set the pace and Moses Calhoun struggled to keep up. There was a long stretch where the two men saw each other less frequently. The sound of a gun or maybe the smell of smoke might alert one to the other's presence, and they would spend just a day or two hunting together.

But for all the time the two men had spent together, Moses never knew that Eli Simmons had a daughter. Or even a wife, for that matter.

"She was a Snake woman," Eli Simmons explained. "A pretty little gal who didn't nag me overmuch. But when our daughter was about ten years old, my wife died. I didn't have no notion of how to go about raising a girl, and so I took her to be with her mother's people."

"Have you seen her since?" Moses Calhoun asked.

"Oh, sure," Eli Simmons said. "I've seen her at times, when I was passing through their camps. She'll be at the winter camp now."

Moses Calhoun took a deep breath, the air almost painful it was so cold. There would certainly be rain and likely be snow before dawn, and it might be a heavy snow.

"We should move on," he said.

The two men continued along their way, coming to the place of Calhoun's promised climb. The grade was steep in places, but Calhoun followed a switchback pattern that made it manageable. Several times the old man had to reach out with his Lancaster rifle and touch Calhoun on the arm, too out of breath to call for a pause. In those times Calhoun kindly stood until he heard the old man's breathing level out. "Ready?" he would ask, and when Eli Simmons confirmed he could keep going, they would resume their climb.

As they neared the top of the ridge, the spruce were so thick that the branches lashed the men in the faces and on the arms as they pushed through.

"A man should have a good trail to his home so that he doesn't come over the threshold all whipped like a dang mule," Eli Simmons complained.

Moses Calhoun laughed at the old man's grumblings.

"There was a time, I remember, when you told me to always alter my route home so as to make sure that there was no trail leading to my door."

"True enough," Eli Simmons said. "But I was younger

then, and had different opinions on things."

They smelled the wood fire before they could see the cabin. As the smell of smoke grew stronger, they at last entered a large meadow on top of a ridge, and at the far end of the meadow, tucked among the spruce trees there, they saw a small light glowing ahead.

"We're home," Moses Calhoun said.

"Who has the fire going?" Eli Simmons asked.

"Kee Kuttai," Calhoun said.

"You take a wife?"

"I did. She's been with me through the last few winters."

"Snake woman?" Old Eli asked.

"Part Snake. Part French-Canadian trapper. She never knew her mother's people, so maybe it weren't Snake. Raised by the Frenchman and his Indian wife, anyway."

"She have any English?"

"Far more than she cares to let on," Calhoun said. "She has more French than English, but we make do."

"Is she a large woman?" Eli Simmons asked. "I always found I preferred a large woman in the winter time."

Moses Calhoun did not answer the question, feeling it was too indecent to answer. A man who lives alone in the mountains too long can forget himself and run away with his mouth.

As they passed through the meadow, rain began to spill upon them, mixed with sleet. The sleet pattered off the wide brim of Calhoun's hat.

"I'll be more glad for that shelter than I expected," Old Eli Simmons said.

As they neared the cabin, the cur dog with the black mouth started barking from inside. In a small paddock near the cabin, a sorrel horse gave a half-interested turn of the head and then ignored the approaching men.

***

Kee Kuttai appeared perturbed to see the old man with her white husband when the two men entered the small log cabin. The dog had alerted her to the men coming through the meadow, and she had fetched down the musket from over the stone fireplace as insurance against thieves – or worse. When Moses Calhoun pulled open the heavy wooden door hung on several leather straps, and pushed past the large bearskin hanging in front of the threshold he was greeted with a musket barrel in his face. He grinned at his wife.

Kee Kuttai saw her husband and returned the musket to its place, lowering the flintlock slowly so that it did not spark. Moses did not speak to the woman. He held the bearskin so that Eli Simmons could step in.

The woman's eyes flashed from Moses to Eli and back.

"Eli Simmons," Moses Calhoun said with a nod to the man. "He is my friend. Mon ami."

Kee Kuttai nodded. Moses grinned at her again. She understood and spoke far more English than she cared to show, especially in front of a stranger.

On the hearth she had a dutch oven and she now

wadded up her apron and lifted the lid.

"Souper?" she asked, making the word sound something in between the French pronunciation and Moses Calhoun's North Carolina twang.

"We et some speared bacon slices, but for myself, I could eat again."

The chimney fire was large and gave off tremendous warmth. There were several stumps of candle burning around the cabin. Both men stripped out of their heavy garments, though old Eli Simmons left his beaverskin hat in place. Moses Calhoun mounted his Tennessee rifle on its hooks above the musket. Kee Kuttai ladled stew from the dutch oven to bowls for the men. She then cut them both a slice of bread.

The cabin was not very large. Moses Calhoun had felled the trees and built the cabin himself, and to spare his back he'd favored a small cabin. The floor was wood slats with gaps that let the air in, but bear skins covered most of the floor. Eli noted that Moses had done a thorough job with the chinking so that all the walls were tight. There were small square windows in three walls, and a door in the fourth wall. The windows were not too large, about big enough for a man to aim and shoot through, and not much bigger. The shutters on two of the windows were closed and covered over with skins, but the third window was open to the elements. That was the light they had seen from across the meadow. The fire put off so much heat that an open window, even in such cold weather, was not inappropriate.

Moses Calhoun was pulling off his boots and socks again and laying them on the hearth near the fire.

"Very cozy," Eli said.

He glanced up at the loft in the gable and was surprised to see the faces of two children looking down at him. Brown haired, both of them, they looked at him with big brown eyes they inherited from their mother.

"You've got young'uns," Eli commented.

Moses Calhoun looked up at the two faces looking down and smiled at his sons.

"Daniel on the left and Elijah on the right," he said. The older boy looked to be about seven years old. The younger one four, maybe five.

"Pleased to meet the both of you," Eli Simmons said. "Elijah, huh? That's the same name as mine."

The small boy smiled and then went to hiding under his blanket.

Eli Simmons looked around the place and felt more than a twinge of jealousy. He'd known many white men in these mountains who took a squaw bride, but those seldom had the appearance anything like what regular folks would recognize as a marriage. Most often, the women were put to hard use – rough use – and a pregnant woman might be sent back to her people, or worse.

But here was Moses Calhoun living a regular sort of life with his Indian woman, and they had two children. Two boys.

"You've got a life here, don't you, young man?" Eli said.

"It's a life, yes," Moses Calhoun said. "Eat now, before the stew gets cold."

The square table had just two short benches on it, but Moses slid to one end and made room for Kee Kuttai to sit beside him when she finished putting stew in a bowl for herself. Eli took the bench opposite them.

"Boys, come and eat your supper," Moses said to them.

"We've already et, Pa," the older boy said. Young Elijah was still hiding beneath his blanket.

Moses Calhoun went after his stew with gusto. Eli believed him when he said he'd not eaten all day, and a slice of bacon wasn't likely to do more than increase his appetite. Eli ate gratefully, but tried to mind his manners, finding himself in the lap of civilization the way he had.

When he'd had several spoonfuls of the stew, Moses sat up and wiped his mouth on his shirtsleeve.

"So you're bound for the Snake winter camp?" Moses asked.

"I am," Eli Simmons said.

Moses scraped his spoon against his bowl and took another bite of food. The stew was a red meat, probably venison, with potatoes and cabbage, carrots and onions, and some bought-flour to stiffen it up.

"This is mighty tasty," Eli Simmons said.

Moses grinned at him.

"We've been friends a long time," Moses said. "We've hunted together many times, through frozen winters and spring thaws. I've seen you get drunk and fall in a stream."

Eli Simmons chuckled, wondering if they were both recalling the same memory or separate occasions.

"I've seen you get scared half to death by a band of Injun warriors."

"That's true," Eli said. "And grizz, too."

"I've seen that," Moses said. "And I've seen you shoot a rabbit at two hundred yards with that Lancaster rifle, and miss a buffalo at sixty yards."

Eli Simmons laughed heartily. "You've never seen me miss no buff at sixty yards.," he said.

"But in all that time, do you know what I've never seen?" Moses said, and there was a serious look on his face that left Eli Simmons feeling uncomfortable.

"What have you never seen, Mose?"

"I ain't never seen you get so lost as you are right now," Moses Calhoun said.

Eli Simmons tapped his spoon against the wooden bowl. Then he scraped the bowl and took another bite, not lifting his eyes. It was several moments of uncomfortable silence.

Kee Kuttai looked from one man to the other and back again. She felt the tension without understanding it.

"Am I so lost?" Eli said at last.

Moses Calhoun nodded sternly.

"You're two hundred miles or more south of the Snake Peoples' winter camp, and if you came from the town, then I make it about thirty miles out of your way that you've come. Is that about right?"

"Maybe not more than twenty," Eli Simmons said, his eyes still turned down, and he feeling chastised.

"Thirty miles," Moses said definitively. "And you built up a fire in that valley that would have attracted a man from five miles away. Other than once or twice when you fell into a stream and near to froze yourself, I don't recollect you being so fond of a fire."

Now Eli Simmons looked up from his bowl. Kee Kuttai and Moses Calhoun were both watching him. She wore an expression of bewilderment, but Moses Calhoun's brow was furrowed in suspicion.

"Fess up," Moses said.

Eli nodded.

"Might as well," he said. "You've caught me, sure enough. Everything I've told you has some truth to it. But I am indeed out of my way, and I am not lost. I came looking for you."

Moses did not speak. He just sat with his eyes on his old friend.

"There is no way I could make it to the winter camp in time," he said. "The soldiers are coming mounted. You saw how I struggled just to get here to your cabin. By the time I could get to the Snake encampment, I'd find nothing there but bodies to bury."

"Qu'est-ce que c'est?" Kee Kuttai asked, looking at her husband for an explanation.

"Old Eli has a daughter with the People," Moses Calhoun said. "The white soldiers are on their way to the winter camp, and Eli fears for his daughter's life."

Kee Kuttai looked back at Eli Simmons, and then to her husband.

"But what has this to do with us?" she asked.

Moses Calhoun gave his old friend a hard look.

"What has this to do with us?" he asked.

Eli Simmons sat up as straight as his old back would allow. His hand trembled slightly, so he set down his spoon and pressed his hand flat against the tabletop.

"I've come to beg a favor," he said.

"No," Moses Calhoun said. "I have a wife and children to look after."

"There'd be no trouble for you," Eli Simmons said quickly. "The Snake People know you. Tekaiten Toi-yah'-to'-ko, they call you."

"There'd be trouble enough if the soldiers caught me," Moses said. "I've no fight with either side, whites nor Indians, and I'll not choose a side by involving myself."

Eli Simmons reached inside his shirt and withdrew a small leather pouch. He set it on the table and it fell heavy with rattling coins.

"It's all I have," he said. "Silver coins, and a couple of gold'uns, too. Every bit of what I have. I'll pay you."

"I don't want your money, Eli," Moses Calhoun said.

The old man's clear blue eyes appeared deeply desperate in the cabin's light, and his voice took on a tone of desperation. He spoke rapidly, pleading.

"She's my daughter, Moses," Eli said. "She has children, barely older than your own. All now waiting to be murdered. I would not ask if there was another way, but there is no other way. I could never clear the distance before the soldiers. But you. You could be there and home again before the soldiers ever arrived. And I ain't asking you to warn the whole camp. Just find my daughter, Aka Ne'ai, and give her my warning. If she chooses to stay, then so be it. And if she chooses to take her young'uns and leave, then all the better. But I'd give you no obligation beyond simply conveying my warning.

I ask as a friend, to the only true friend I've ever had."

Moses glanced at his children in the loft. They were hanging their heads over the side, listening to every word that was spoken. He looked at his wife, her large, dark eyes full of worry.

"I cannot leave my family," he said. "I wish I could help you, but I cannot."

"Then I will have to make an early start of it in the morning," Eli Simmons said. "I must at least try."

Eli Simmons made a bed of bear skins and blankets on the floor. He'd slept many a night in worse conditions. Moses Calhoun pulled closed the open shutters, and he and Kee Kuttai climbed into the loft and slept with their children between them.

- 2 -

Private Chris Dolan had tied two pieces of twine over the top of his hat and under his chin, but he now worried that the wind would catch up under his hat like a sail and rip his head right off of his shoulders.

Pvt. Dolan felt that he would freeze atop his horse in the early dawn with the cold wind blowing into his face, and the thought made him angrier than ever because this was not what he volunteered for.

Thirteen men, including Lt. Fisher and Sgt. Terry, rode ahead of him, and another ten men rode behind. The twenty-four men left the fort four days ago. They were the last of the detachments to leave over the course of the past two months. Each detachment rode out of the fort to give the appearance of riding on patrol or some other specific purpose. But for weeks troopers had been leaving the fort and not returning.

Lieutenant Fisher knew, and maybe Sergeant Terry, but the men could only speculate. No one bothered to tell them anything.

Hep Chandler, who like Dolan was a volunteer from California, had surmised they were going to strike against the Indians. Which was fine. Anything was better than the endless days of boredom at the fort or the meaningless patrols along the trail. The most any of the California volunteers could say they had done was to protect prospectors heading north into the mountains, but the volunteers knew they'd done no such thing. For all the patrols and all the skirmishes with Indians, the California boys had engaged in, prospectors and homesteaders heading along the trails were still being ambushed and slaughtered.

It seemed that once a week someone rode into the fort with another story of dead white men on the trails. And sometimes it was families killed.

Dolan, like the other volunteers, had signed on to go east and kill the Southern rebels.

Instead, the War Department had seen fit to bivouac them in the frozen Northwest to deal with Indians. But other than a few skirmishes that mostly ended with no one dead and the Indians disappearing into the hills, the volunteers weren't even accomplishing that.

"I reckon we're going to be a mite disappointed when we finally get wherever we're going," Hep Chandler shouted into the wind.

Dolan turned in his saddle and looked back at Hep. Hep had tied his hat to his head with a neckerchief to try to protect his ears. His wind-burnt face looked painfully cold. Still, Hep managed a wry smile.

"Why's that?" Chris Dolan asked.

"We signed on to kill Rebel traitors, but I reckon there ain't no Johnny Rebs this far north," Hep said.

Private Dolan was too cold to laugh, so he just turned back in his saddle and kept riding.

The boys were all itching for a fight, and they would fight Indians if they couldn't fight traitors.

Billy Douglas said he'd rather fight Indians anyhow, and that was a sentiment that had taken root among the volunteers in recent weeks.

The men rode through the morning with the cold wind whipping at them on the open plains, and early in the afternoon they stopped to rest their horses and took shelter from the wind in a dry creek bed.

Lieutenant Webb Fisher led the patrol of two-dozen men. Fisher graduated West Point, but it was said among the men that he did so poorly that the War Department stationed him out West because he was not even fit to stop a Rebel bullet. All Chris Dolan knew for certain was that Webb Fisher was the oldest lieutenant he'd ever seen. He also had little use for army discipline unless he was angry at a trooper, and then he'd have the man whipped or punished in some other way. The man was also given to drink on a regular basis, and even on patrol carried a flask from which he drank liberally.

"Lieutenant, we've been gone from the fort for four

days and we're not turning back," Hep Chandler said as the men milled about while their horses grazed. "Where are we bound for?"

Lieutenant Fisher chewed some jerky and studied Hep Chandler for a while.

Hep and Chris Dolan's older brother Craig had been friends from childhood, and Chris had always followed the two of them around. When they were little, he followed them everywhere, and often as not was coaxed into doing their chores for them. When they decided to leave their family farms in Illinois and go to California to dig for gold, Chris went with them. In California, when they decided to enlist to go kill Southern Rebels, Chris went with them. He'd always admired Hep, who had an easy way and was quick to make a joke. But he worshiped his older brother Craig. Craig Dolan was the third son in a family of eight children. Chris was the youngest of the lot, and Craig was two years older.

Craig decided at 18 that he would have to make his own way in life. The farm was big enough to support the two oldest boys, but it would never do for Craig and Chris. With Hep, he settled on going to California, much against his father's wishes. Maybe the greatest day of Chris's life was when Craig and Hep asked him to come along.

Craig and Chris made pretty good troopers. They followed orders, didn't gripe more than anyone else, and they kept their heads down.

Hep Chandler was not so good at soldiering.

He complained loudly and often. He questioned orders frequently. But somehow, he'd fallen into Lieutenant Fisher's good graces, and the lieutenant accepted an awful lot from Hep that would have got any of the others a reprimand or maybe a lashing.

"Why do you always got to know everything?" Lieutenant Chandler said, digging a piece of jerky from between his teeth with his little finger's nail.

"I just like to know where I'm bound, and for what purpose," Hep said.

Lieutenant Fisher sucked at his teeth noisily, and then went back to work with his fingernail.

"Well, it's like this, Chandler. You've seen them mountains on the horizon, haven't you?"

"Sure."

"We're going up into them mountains to teach the Red Man a lesson he'll not soon forget," Lieutenant Fisher said. "I reckon there's no point in keeping it hid. The colonel's been dispatching troopers for two months to keep it quiet, sending out patrols hither and yon. We're all to rendezvous tomorrow, and then the regiment is riding into the mountains to get after them Injuns for what they done to them settlers back in the spring."

Lieutenant Fisher did not need to elaborate.

There had been many attacks in the last few years. Folks said the Indians were growing bolder because they knew the armies were off fighting in the east. Some opined that the Indians were getting more ruthless because the encroachment on their traditional hunting grounds was starving them out.

Either way, back in the spring the Indians laid upon a small band of wagons, families of homesteaders bound for the valley of the Walla Walla.

The stories that came back to the fort were horrible. Grown men wept.

Other settlers found the bodies and turned back for help. Folks in a nearby town, seeing the site, sent to the fort. A detachment of soldiers rode up to the site and patrolled the area, but never could find the Indians that did it.

The homesteaders had been tortured and mutilated for the entertainment of the Indians who did it. A young girl's legs were amputated, and they said that evidence at the scene suggested she was made to walk upon the stumps. That was not the worst of it, either.

It turned Chris Dolan's stomach to even think of what had been done to them poor families.

"Well, it's about time we're doing something useful," Hep Chandler said.

"Amen to that," another of the troopers said.

Some months ago, back in the previous winter, the men at the fort all signed a petition to the War Department to send them to the Army of the Potomac. They'd signed on to fight, and all they were doing was huddling under blankets in a fort in the middle of nowhere. The petition offered to have their wages withheld to pay for their transportation to the Eastern Theater.

Everyone was itching for a fight, and if it couldn't be with Southrons, then they would be happy to fight Indians.

"So that's why we're campaigning this late in the year?" Craig Dolan asked.

"That's why," Lieutenant Fisher said. "We're going to catch them in their winter camp so they can't go slipping off from us like they have before."

The lieutenant examined his fingernail and flicked a small piece of grizzle off of it, then slid his hand back into his gauntlet. He gave Sergeant Clay Terry a nod, and the sergeant stood up.

"All right, men. Mount up!"

The troopers resumed their horses and single-file continued their trek north to rendezvous with the rest of their regiment.

- 3 -

Dawn came with a heavy fog and a layer of frost on the ground, but the snow Moses Calhoun expected to find was not there.

"Go to the smokehouse and cut a side of venison," Moses Calhoun told Kee Kuttai. Then turning to Eli Simmons, he said, "I'll give you my canteen, and the meat, to help get you along."

"I'll move faster without them," Eli Simmons said.

Moses watched the old man struggle with his boots. His feet and ankles were swollen.

"How long did it take you to get here from the town?" Moses asked.

Eli Simmons shrugged.

"Three days was all."

Moses could make it to the town in two days if he was in a hurry.

"Too bad about your mule," Moses said. It was a searching question. He'd never believed that Eli Simmons lost a mule to a bear.

"There warn't no mule," Eli Simmons confessed. "I hated to admit that I lost my canteen off a cliff. I set down on a rock over a ravine, and set my canteen beside me. Damned if it didn't slide into oblivion."

Moses Calhoun frowned.

"Well, you can take mine," he said.

Without another word, he stood up and put on his coat and walked outside after his wife.

The smokehouse was a poor excuse, but it served the purpose. It was, in fact, Moses Calhoun's first cabin built in these mountains – not tall enough for him to stand erect, barely wide enough for him to lie down stretched out. But it had gotten him through his first two winters in the mountains, and it had made for a serviceable smokehouse when he finished building his current cabin. They had sides of venison and bear meat hanging in the smokehouse, and Calhoun inhaled the smell of smoked meat coming from the open door as he approached. Along with the vegetables from their kitchen garden, the meat inside the smokehouse was what would keep Calhoun and his family alive through the coming winter.

A horse in the corral snorted as Calhoun passed

near, its breath hanging like puffs of smoke in front of its nostrils.

He found Kee Kuttai in the smokehouse.

"I'm going to go," he said.

She shut her eyes and took a heavy breath.

"I wish you would not," she said. "Snow will be coming soon."

"Ten days, not more than twelve," Moses said. "I'll be home before it's a heavy snow. But Old Eli, he can't make it to the Indian camp. Not in time."

"You do not owe that man anything," Kee Kuttai said. "But you owe me and you owe your children. If you do not come back, how do we survive?"

"You've meat and vegetables stored up enough to see you through the winter," Moses Calhoun said. "Plenty of cut wood for fires. In the spring, you take the children and go to the town."

The woman shook her head sadly, but she made no more argument.

Moses walked back into the cabin. Eli Simmons was tying leather thongs around the tops of his boots to keep the water out.

"I'll go and find your daughter," Moses said. Eli looked up sharply but did not respond. "You go on back to the town before the snow comes. I've got an old mule I can lend you that you can ride back. I know about where the Snake have set up their winter camp, and I can find your daughter. I'll deliver the warning to her, like you asked, but I won't promise more than that."

"Aka Ne'ai," Eli Simmons said. "Sunflower Wind. She can speak English just fine. You send her to find me, and

35

I'll take care of her and her husband and their children through the winter. You tell her that."

Moses nodded.

"I'm grateful to you Calhoun," Eli said. "You keep that money purse."

The younger man shook his head.

"You don't pay a friend for a favor. If your daughter turns up with her children, you'll need the money to see them through the winter."

Eli dropped his head.

"I'm not the sort of man who comes easy to ask a favor like this," he said. "But it's a thing I just can't do for myself. I can't get to the Snake People before the soldiers. Not as slow as I move these days."

Moses Calhoun patted the man on his arm.

"Tell me your daughter's name again," Calhoun said.

"Aka Ne'ai," Eli said. "Her husband is Kee Nangkawitsi Tekaiten. Last I saw them, the children weren't named yet. But Kee Nangkawitsi Tekaiten follows the Chief Mukuakantun. I believe you know him."

"I know him," Moses Calhoun said, though it was not necessary to confirm it. Eli Simmons knew well enough that Moses Calhoun was acquainted with Mukuakantun.

At one time the tribe moved mostly as one, but the past few years when the spring thaw came, the tribe drifted in small bands in separate ways, coming together again in large bands in the winter camps. The press of emigrants, trappers and hunters, and war with other tribes had pushed the Snake People to the brink of starvation. And so they split into smaller groups to forage for the spring and summer months.

Chief Mukuakantun was a leader in his tribe, and Moses Calhoun knew him to be a peaceful man. But like others in his tribe, he had taken to theft to feed his tribe. The white settlers in the area despised the Indians, but Moses Calhoun found it hard to condemn a man for doing what he had to do to feed his children.

Having made his decision to go, Moses Calhoun did not waste time.

He fetched from his corral a horse and a mule for himself and a mule for Eli Simmons.

"He's old, and doesn't move so fast, but he's still sure-footed and will get you back to town," Moses said.

"We'll be a matched pair," Eli said. "I'll return him to you in the spring."

Moses shrugged.

"If he's useful to you, don't worry about bringing him back."

He had no extra saddle.

"I've never been so fancy as to need a saddle," Eli said. "An old blanket and a rope halter, and this mule and I will be like old chums."

He saw the old man off with one last promise to get word to Aka Ne'ai.

When Eli Simmons was on his way, Moses hurried to get his things together. He packed shot and powder and provisions enough to see him through several days. He packed his heavy bearskin coat and a wool blanket for the nights.

Kee Kuttai saddled the horse, a sorrel with a white blaze on his face, while Moses finished packing the mule.

In less than a half hour, he was ready to go. Just inside the door of the cabin, Moses put his arms around his wife and held her close to him. Her eyes were filled with water, but she locked an impassive look on her face, refusing to let Moses see her weakness for him.

"Depeche-toi," she said, touching his bearded cheek.

"Oui," he said. "I will be back so soon you'll not have time to miss me."

The two boys watched the scene from the back of the cabin until at last Daniel, the older of the two, could stand it no longer. He rushed forward, tears in his eyes. He did not understand what his father was doing, but he understood the tension the old man with the heavy white beard had brought to the house. He understood, too, the tears in his mother's eyes.

"Papa!" Daniel said, his arms outstretched. "Papa!"

The boy sprang forward and Moses Calhoun caught him in mid-air and brought him to an embrace.

"Papa, let me go with you!"

Moses hugged his son and patted his head.

"Next time," he said. "This time I have to make tracks quickly. But next time, when there is no rush, you will go with me."

Elijah, as confused as his brother, declined an invitation to hug his father, but Moses walked over and picked up the boy, giving him an embrace. "You help your brother take care of ta mere."

The boy nodded but did not speak.

Moses Calhoun mounted the sorrel and took the lead rope of the mule. Kee Kuttai walked outside with him and patted the horse's neck.

On his belt he carried a sturdy Bowie knife. His long rifle was packed with the supplies on the mule. Tucked into the straps of his saddle was a short hatchet with a bladed cutting edge on one side and a metal ball on the other that could be used for clubbing an enemy. In his life, Moses Calhoun had found few opportunities to need a weapon to defend himself, but when those opportunities came, he always proved capable of meeting the challenge. But he knew with soldiers near and the Snake People threatened, anything could happen, so he did not set out unprepared.

***

Moses Calhoun followed a trail he'd taken many times down into the valley below his cabin, and he set out to the northwest through that valley.

Once he was down off the spruce- and aspen-covered slope, Moses found it to be easy going through the grassy meadow. He was protected from the vicious cold of the winds by the high stone hills surrounding the valley, and the sun had come out and pleasantly warmed the day. A gentle stream flowed through the bottom of the valley, and Moses rode near that stream. Come spring, with the snow melt, that stream would rage as the water rushed down from the mountains, but for now it was a flat, gently rolling creek.

The sorrel kept a good trot going, and the mule was not so overburdened that he refused to keep up, and so Moses Calhoun managed to make good time. He'd come through this valley at times when the snow was so deep, he could see the camp he left in the morning when he stopped to camp at night. He'd also come through it when the rains had been so heavy that it was all he could do to keep his horse from getting mired. But the valley was also his greatest source of food. In the summertime and early autumn, Moses could sit from dawn to dusk, waiting for a deer or moose to cross through the valley and be assured that before dark he would have meat for the smokehouse.

He rode all day without seeing much that interested him. By late morning, the mule had turned stubborn and wouldn't give anything more than a walk. But they had two hundred miles or more to cover, and Moses did not try to force the issue. Their pace slowed considerably, but he still covered a good distance.

He stayed in the meadow, skirting the places where the spruce forests seemed to spill off the mountainsides into the valley.

In the afternoon he saw a small herd of pronghorn far ahead of him in the meadow.

They were too far off to make a good shot, and he didn't need to take one anyway. He had meat enough in his pack on the mule. If he were closer to the Snake People's winter camp, he might have shot and cleaned one of the pronghorn to offer as a gift, but he still had too far to go to be thinking about bringing gifts.

He camped among the spruce trees that night.

He made a shelter of spruce branches and a fire just big enough to boil water for coffee and to heat his meat in a pan. He did not worry overmuch about Indians, though a man alone in these mountains could never be too cautious about Indians, but it was always a fear that a campfire might draw a bear or a big cat.

Moses Calhoun picketed the horse and mule close to

his shelter, knowing they would sense danger and alert him to it.

The shelter did nothing to keep back the cold, and the fire stayed too low and burned out before it was useful for warmth. The seasoned hunter was accustomed, though, to cold nights spent in a makeshift shelter, and under his heavy bearskin coat and wool blanket, he slept well enough.

He was awake before first light. The valley was covered in a thick fog, and the morning air chilled him to the bone when he emerged from his blankets and shelter.

Calhoun gathered up some small sticks he had collected the night before and bent low over his fire, brushing away the cold ash until he found some warm embers buried deep beneath. He held twigs with dry spruce needles down against the embers and blew air until the needles caught and he had a small flame.

He moved more twigs with needles against the first, and those caught. Quickly, he added more twigs until he had a small fire started, and then he began to lay small sticks into the flames, continuing to give a little air to the fire until the sticks began to catch. Soon he had a fire of a decent size going.

His horse and mule watched him with interest, though it was nothing they'd not seen before.

He did not worry now about the size of the fire, and he built it up enough to provide him with some warmth against the morning cold.

Then he made coffee and cooked himself a breakfast.

Kee Kuttai had packed him some hard biscuits, and he cooked the meat in his pan and then split one of the biscuits, cooking it with the doughy inside down in the grease. He cut a raw potato in half and then sliced several thin pieces that he dropped down into the grease to cook as well.

It wasn't much of a meal, perhaps, but Moses Calhoun found great pleasure in a breakfast cooked over an open fire on a cold morning. The warmth of the flames and hot coals seemed to soak into his body, and he accepted it gratefully.

By the time the first light of morning appeared in the sky over the canopy of spruce trees, Moses Calhoun had eaten his breakfast and stomped down his fire, kicking dirt over it. He packed the mule, but left his bearskin coat on. He would wait until the sun was well up before abandoning the coat for the day.

He left his shelter in place. A man never knew when someone else in a few days or weeks might come along and find that shelter could mean the difference between surviving the night or not, and so Moses always left his shelters standing.

And then he was mounted again, picking his way among the spruce trees, back down into the open meadow.

He figured he'd made forty miles the first day.

"If the weather holds, we'll be home in fewer than twelve days," he promised the sorrel and the mule.

- 4 -

Lieutenant Fisher's patrol arrived at the rendezvous on the same day that the scouts returned with a positive location of the Snake People's winter camp.

A full regiment came to twelve companies, each company had between eighty and one hundred men. But the group rendezvousing consisted of just four companies so that the regiment going to punish the Indians came to just under four hundred troopers riding under the command of a Colonel Culberson. They called Culberson's men a "regiment," though the total number of men fell fall short of a full regiment.

With their tents lined in a valley outside of the small town, the men seemed to be an enormous army, not just a handful of companies.

Their arms were stacked out front of the tents, and the tents were organized in impressive grids that seemed to line up perfectly.

As they rode into the encampment, Sergeant Terry shook his head in disgust.

"All these men and all this gear, it'll be summer before we get to the Injuns' winter camp, and they'll be gone," he said under his breath.

"Surely we won't take all this gear?" Craig Dolan asked.

"You haven't been in the army long enough, son," Terry said. "We've got majors and captains and lieutenants in this regiment, and they can't be expected to travel without tents and desks and a change of clothes for every other day."

Terry spread an arm in grandiose fashion.

"You're looking at the reason we'll never beat the Injuns," he said. "They travel light and move fast. We take the entire city of Baltimore with us everywhere we go."

The men herded their mounts into one of the many makeshift corrals set up and then carried their gear into the camp to wait for orders. Lieutenant Fisher left them to go and find the captain to report their arrival.

As the patrol mingled with other troopers, they learned that some of them had been in camp for a month already. Most everyone was desperate to move, and they all seemed to be repeating Sergeant Terry's complaint.

"Hurry up and wait."

"Inactive."

"The Rebs are bivouacked outside of Washington D.C., and a thousand good fighting men loyal to the Union are twiddling thumbs in the middle of nowhere."

As the day wore on, word began to spread that the scouts had returned and had the location of the winter quarters. Some people swore they would break camp at dawn and head northwest to where the Indians had been found. Others argued that it would take the officers a week to decide to move.

Chris Dolan, his brother, and the rest of their 24-man patrol – excepting the lieutenant – found their tents and set them up on the edge of the tent city. Sergeant Terry complained the entire time, and in his foul mood he made Hep Chandler and Craig Dolan completely take down their tent and set it up again, claiming it was a full foot out of position. Craig did not think it was, nor did Chris, but the two men did as they were told.

At dark, Lieutenant Fisher turned up, and he gathered the twenty-three men who rode in with him. He seemed agitated.

"We're leaving at dawn," he informed them. "The regiment will break camp and start in the morning, but we're riding out ahead of the regiment. We're going with two of the scouts who located the Snake camp, and we're to go to reconnoiter the situation at the winter camp."

The men took the news with a thrill of excitement. Some smiled and nodded to each other, others clenched their jaws in resolute determination. There was a bit of murmuring. But a quick glance around at the others sitting around the campfire, and Chris Dolan could see that, to a man, they all took the news with eager confidence.

"So we're really going, then?" Hep Chandler said.

"Of course we're really going," Lieutenant Fisher snapped. The men all glanced at him, surprised to see him lose patience with Hep Chandler who so often got away with any comment. "You don't think we'd have an entire regiment bivouacked out here in this cold weather and not go?"

Lieutenant Fisher stood up and, in a huff, and walked away from the other men.

"What's his trouble?" Hep asked when Fisher was out of earshot.

Clay Terry, who had been a sergeant in the army for several years, even before the war, grunted. He was roughly the same age as Lieutenant Fisher and had known the officer for a long time. Sergeant Terry was competent and thorough in his military efficiency. He allowed whatever lack of discipline his commanding officer allowed, but the men knew they could count on Terry if things got rough. They'd been in a few minor encounters with Indians, and in those instances, they'd seen Terry's mettle. Most of them considered him to be the man in charge, and not Lieutenant Fisher.

"What?" Hep said to him.

"Don't you worry about what I think," Sergeant Terry said.

"I want to know," Hep pushed him.

"Sure, Sarge," Craig Dolan chimed in. "Tell us what you're thinking."

Sergeant Terry looked around over his shoulder to be sure that no officer, but especially not Lieutenant Fisher, was in earshot.

"I think he doesn't want to be sent out on this duty," Terry said. "That's what I think, and that's all I will say about it."

To prove that he wouldn't say any more, Sergeant Terry got up and left the campfire.

With a cold wind moaning on the outskirts of the tents and the fire burning down, the twenty-two volunteer cavalrymen of K Company who had been given the mission to ride ahead of the rest of the regiment now huddled near to one another and discussed the events of the evening. Excitement, surely, boiled among the half-frozen men, but something else drew most of the attention of the conversation. Sergeant Terry's dismissive attitude toward their lieutenant.

It was no secret that Lieutenant Fisher was a poor officer. The oldest lieutenant in the regiment, he had been consistently passed over for promotion. But now a new word was going around among the men in his small patrol, and it chilled the men who knew they would have to follow him into action.

Cowardice.

- 5 -

Moses Calhoun woke to the nervous snort of his horse.

He did not linger under the heavy blanket, or take a last moment to gird himself against the cold of the night.

His fingers wrapped around the leather-wrapped and beaded handle of his hatchet, and he came out of the shelter he'd made with all his senses sharp and ready for whatever he found out there.

The horse shifted nervously against its lead rope, and Calhoun laid a calming hand on the bay's neck. The mule danced around nervously as well, though now – at Calhoun's presence – both animals calmed some.

The forest at night is alive with a hundred noises. Wind in the branches. An owl seeking prey. A rodent scurrying in the brush.

A thin sliver of moonlight pieced through the spruce canopy, enough so that Calhoun could see the shapes of his horse and mule, the heavy fir branches around him, the black shadow against the darkness in the place where his shelter stood. But he would never see whatever had spooked the horse if it decided to make a meal of him. He would have to hear it coming. His ears were well attuned to the noises of the woods. A rustling in the brush could be distinguished from a small rodent to a large cat. The heavy breathing of a lumbering bear was a sound all its own, and the scream of a big cat at dusk could freeze a man's blood in his veins.

Calhoun stayed still and tried to keep the animals calm as he listened at the night.

Nothing he heard caused him any concern, though he did hear a distant wolf howling.

He was three days out from his cabin now. One more full day of riding, maybe two, and he would find the Snake People's winter camp. The snow had still held off, though the previous afternoon the sky turned gray and the temperature seemed to drop even lower. He doubted that he could be home before the first snow.

Both the horse and the mule remained nervous. Several times the horse snapped its head one direction or another, ears perked and nostrils flared tight.

But Calhoun heard nothing. No movement in the brush, no heavy breathing.

If there was a bear nearby, Calhoun did not want to tempt it by cooking food, so he decided not to start a fire. He would miss the added bit of warmth in the morning, and the coffee, but the smell of meat cooking might prove too much for a bear to resist. He had on his heavy bearskin coat, and that would have to be enough to protect him against the cold.

Calhoun did not bother trying to go back to sleep. His presence seemed to calm the horse and mule, and it was not long before the light of dawn appeared blue in the night sky.

That first light of dawn always appeared high in the sky, and once it shone, morning came on fast. One moment, just the tiniest bit of blue appeared high overhead with blackness all around, and next moment a gray light permeated even into the dense forest.

Calhoun loved mornings, when the veil of darkness lifted. Especially in spring, but even now in the coming of winter, the birds kept up a constant chatter. In the early morning the animals would rise and stretch their legs. The whole country came alive in the mornings.

As the grayness descended from the sky and began to slip all around, Calhoun started to pack his gear. But he had an uneasy feeling.

The horse remained alert, his ears cocked back like the hammer on a gun, his nostrils taut.

And then Moses Calhoun realized that there were no birds singing nearby.

He might have put it down to the lateness of the season. Many birds drifted to warmer environs. But even so, plenty of winter birds remained in the area, and it was uncommon to hear no birds at first light. Neither did he hear squirrels or other small animals.

He'd set his hatchet down beside his makeshift shelter while he packed his gear, and now he reached out for it.

The two things happened at once.

Calhoun's fingertips felt the tiny beads on the leather-bound handle of his hatchet just as he heard an almighty rush through the brush behind him.

The horse gave out a cry and the mule stomped its hind legs.

He knew what it was by instinct.

A lynx or a cougar, one. A big cat had stalked his camp through the night. Now, crouched low to gather his gear from the shelter of spruce boughs, he'd presented an opportunity to the cat.

Calhoun's right hand grasped the handle of the hatchet.

He spun to his left, raising his left arm to protect his head, just as the cat leapt.

He caught the full weight of the cat – a 100-pound mountain lion – and tumbled backwards into the shelter.

The heavy bearskin coat is what saved him. The sharp claws grabbed Calhoun's back and caught his right arm as the lion's jaws set on his left forearm. Though he felt the strength in those claws and in the jaw, the coat, for now, had protected him from serious injury.

Together, hunter and prey tumbled into the shelter, knocking down the boughs as if they were no more than cloth.

They tumbled one over the other, and ended with

the cat on top of Moses Calhoun.

The cougar's jaw was locked on his left arm, and one heavy foot pressed into his chest. But tumbling through the shelter the way they had left the cat unsteady.

Calhoun swung with his right. The heavy metal ball on the backside of hatchet smashed hard into the cougar's head.

Moses felt the jaw clench tighter on his arm. But he felt the heavy claw on his chest release some of its pressure.

He didn't try for a second heavy blow. Instead, he flicked his wrist for a fast, sharp blow that smacked the mountain lion in its head a second time.

Calhoun pulled his left arm closer to him, the lion's face coming so close he could feel the heavy breath from its nostrils against his own face. As he pulled his arm toward himself, the lion pulled against. Its jaws so tight that he thought it might break his forearm. Now, with all his force, he flung himself into the great cat, throwing himself the way the cat was pulling so that man and lion were both going in the same direction.

The cat toppled, and now Moses was free. He found himself on his hands and knees now, instead of his back. The cat, startled to find its prey unexpectedly free, raised up a paw to swipe at him. Calhoun threw a protecting arm over his head and caught the full force of the cat's big paw against his shoulder. It knocked him a terrible blow, but he did not collapse to his stomach.

Now Calhoun swung hard with the hatchet, this time catching the big cat in its side with the blade.

The lion sprang backwards.

Stunned and a bit rattled, Moses Calhoun jumped to his feet. He spread his arms wide to make himself big, raising the hatchet up high over his head.

"I am Tekaiten Toi-yah'-to'-ko!" Calhoun shouted at the lion. "Tekaiten Toi-yah'-to'-ko!"

He shook his arms and took a step toward the mountain lion.

The cat snarled and, though well out of reach, swung a vicious claw into the air.

"Tekaiten Toi-yah'-to'-ko!" Moses shouted again, the hatchet poised above him, ready to strike a fatal blow.

Then it retreated into the brush.

A cold chill ran through Moses Calhoun. He was drenched in sweat, and not from exertion. Calhoun knew of many men who had fallen prey to a grizzly or a black bear. He'd heard of mountain lions killing children, but only a few times. He had never heard of a grown man being killed by a cougar. But something about the attack of a mountain lion gripped him with fear.

It was not the first time Moses Calhoun had been attacked by a predator cat. He seemed to have a knack for wandering into their hunting grounds. Despite the name that he was called by the Snake People, he had never hunted mountain lions and only ever killed one.

Now certain that the lion had given up and gone in search of another meal, Moses Calhoun stripped off his heavy bearskin coat and slid out of his buckskin jacket. He pulled up the sleeve of his shirt and examined his arm. The coat and jacket had kept the cat from puncturing his skin, but the arm was tender and would bruise badly. Thankfully, the bones had not broken.

He pulled his shirt from his pants and raised it so that he could see his chest.

Two shallow gashes where two of the claws had gotten inside his coat. They were not bleeding bad, but they stung. He examined his shirt and found the holes where the claws had ripped through.

He knew he was lucky to have survived without more injury.

What scared Moses Calhoun the most was not death. All men die. But he was afraid for Kee Kuttai and his children and what would happen to them if he was not there to protect and provide for them.

The horse and mule were calm now.

The threat concluded, Moses decided to make a fire and have some coffee. He would be satisfied with a later start than he intended.

- 6 -

Somewhere in the far distance an animal screeched out a blood curdling cry, and Chris Dolan's head shot up. Chris was not alone. Most of the troopers all looked around fearfully.

None of them could even distinguish from which direction it came. Haunting, chilling, it seemed to be all around them.

The Lakota scout grinned at their fear.

They called him "Jack Cut Face," though all the troopers suspected that was not his given name. He was full-blooded Lakota. His face bore a deep scar from hairline to jaw where he had been sliced with a hatchet, a gift from a Snake warrior.

Jack Cut Face did not speak much to the soldiers. Chris Dolan had the sense that he despised them, which was true enough. But his people had been at war with the Snake People for more years than Jack Cut Face knew, and he hated the Snake People more than he hated the white soldiers. And so he would help the white soldiers find the Snake People in their winter camp and be pleased with the deaths on both sides.

The other scout was an old trapper called Bearclaw Jim. Gray-headed and gray-bearded, he had a harsh voice from the damage a bear had done when it swiped at his neck. He killed that bear with his Arkansas toothpick and then made a necklace of its claws so they would always be near the place they had last drawn blood. He'd been a younger man, then, and much stronger. Now it was a strain just to stand and walk. But he endured the discomfort because there was nothing else to do.

When the soldiers all cocked their heads, Bearclaw Jim let out a hardy cackle.

"Mountain lion," he explained to them when he was done laughing at their fright.

"Where is it?" Billy Douglas asked.

"Nowhere near us," Bearclaw Jim said. "It sounds like he's just lost a fight with a bigger cat. Probably disappointed he ain't got no breakfast."

Bearclaw Jim cackled another laugh.

They'd camped in a wide meadow and built up a good-sized fire that burned through the night. The men carried blankets, but no tents. They were to move light and fast so that they could get near the Snake camp, identify the best routes of attack, and then report back to the main body of the regiment moving slowly behind them.

Lieutenant Fisher had no interest in the mountain lion or his men's fright.

"How much farther to the camp?" he asked Bearclaw Jim.

Fisher despised the old trapper, but he would not deign to speak to the Indian.

"Two days out," he said. "As long as a pack of mountain lions don't get us."

He cackled some more at the wary looks among the troopers.

"They don't travel in packs," Hep Chandler said.

"That's what you know," Bearclaw Jim said. "But I reckon I've seen more in these mountains than you've ever seen. You ever see a pack of lions, it'll be the last you ever see."

Disgusted by the trapper and incensed to be so far out on his own, Lieutenant Fisher stood up and touched the toe of his boot against Sergeant Terry's leg.

"Let's get moving," he said. "The faster we get to the camp and have a look, the faster we can get back to the regiment."

"What's the matter, General?" Bearclaw Jim said. "Don't you worry none about them Snake warriors. They all half-starved."

Lieutenant Fisher turned on Bearclaw Jim. He raised up a gloved-hand and swiped it down hard, back-handing Bearclaw Jim across the face. The old trapper's neck snapped.

"Watch how you address me," Fisher said, his face red with fury. "'Lieutenant Fisher' and 'sir.' Address me familiar, or call me 'general' again, and I'll have you tied to a tree and your back scraped clean. Do you understand me?"

Bearclaw Jim narrowed his eyes, and every man present could see the venom on his face.

"Yes, sir," he said, biting off the words.

For Bearclaw Jim, scouting for the army was the lowest way of earning a wage, and he despised doing it. But he couldn't get around so well these days. Running traps was too much work on his back. Skinning and gutting, it was all too strenuous. It was about all he could do to mount a horse and spend the day in a saddle. He hated the army and hated the soldiers. It took a certain kind of man to be a soldier – the sort of man who would spend all day being told what to do – and Bearclaw Jim couldn't respect that lack of spirit.

Sergeant Terry got to his feet and started directing the troopers to get their gear together and get on the move.

The men were frozen. Their wool coats did little to protect them from the cold that had descended on them in the last two days. The gray clouds overhead seemed to press the cold down on them. At least the wind here in the valley was considerably less than what they'd been through on the plains, but cold seemed to cut right through them.

"Get your horses saddled and be fast about it," Sergeant Terry ordered them.

The sun never shone all day. The gray clouds held

fast, pushing down the cold. The wind picked up a bit, swaying the spruce up and down the surrounding slopes. The men clutched their wool coats closed at the throat to try to keep their body heat inside their clothes as they walked their horses deeper into the mountains.

Chris Dolan was sure this was misery.

He missed the camaraderie they had at the fort. Back at the fort it was more like it had been in California at the diggings. The men were constantly joking, and even in their boredom they were full of life. But here, in these frozen mountains with the frost crunching under the weight of their horses, the men seemed tired and grumpy. Even Hep Chandler had no jokes to tell.

And the worst part of it was the constant feeling that in the thick forests there were unseen eyes watching them.

Chris Dolan didn't know if it was Indians or bears or mountain lions, but he felt certain that someone or something was always watching them, stalking them.

He felt that the scouts should do something about it. The Lakota, if not the old trapper, should be aware that they were being watched. But he hadn't made mention of it. He hadn't ridden up onto the slopes to find what was on them. He hadn't issued a warning to Lieutenant Fisher.

Chris Dolan didn't say anything to any of the other troopers about his fears. He didn't want them to tease him for being afraid, but he wondered if they didn't feel it, too.

He would have much preferred to be with the regiment. Riding with four hundred men did a lot to allay fears. But riding with just a few men, going toward an encampment of hundreds of enemies in a hostile environment – Private Chris Dolan swallowed hard and cinched up on his reins. He squeezed the collar of his coat tighter against his body.

He was cold and miserable.

- 7 -

The first flakes of snow began to fall in the early afternoon – big, heavy flakes that seemed determined. With the sun staying behind the clouds, the frost on the ground never truly thawed, and Moses Calhoun knew that the snow would stick. The darkness of the clouds suggested that it would be more than just a dusting.

The mule seemed to stiffen up with the snow. He was harder to get moving and slower once he was going.

He was approaching the hardest part of his journey where he would have to leave the meadow in the valley and cut up through a mountain pass. He'd been through here before, and had hoped that he would get to the pass before dark. But the mule's stubborn attitude and his own lingering that morning had ensured he wouldn't make the pass today.

The snow kept coming. It fell in flakes on his buckskin shirt. At first the flakes turned to water and slid off, but now he found the flakes stayed and accumulated on his arm and he had to brush them away. He felt cold inside his clothes, but he did not stop to put on his heavier coat. He liked that it provided him with more warmth after dark.

Late in the afternoon, Moses Calhoun found himself on a switchback trail up a big slope. The pass was a saddle between two high mountains, but he would have to climb just to get there. The trail was deep in a forest of spruce and tall lodgepole pines, and here the snow did not reach the ground. But he could look up through the canopy and see that it was still coming down.

Maybe the sun would rally and come out in a day or two and melt off this first snow. It usually did. It would leave everything wet but warmer.

He did not regret making a promise to Eli Simmons. Old Elijah would have never made it. Not before the soldiers. And if he'd encountered that mountain lion, he might not have made it any farther than that.

As he slowly ascended the trail, Moses became aware of the scent of smoke on the air. It smelled strong, not like a campfire but like a chimney fire. The smell surprised him. This wasn't an area where settler or even trappers were known to stay. During the warm months, this was Snake hunting territory and dangerous for a white man. But when the trail came to a long ridge,

Moses followed the smell until he at last came to a cabin sitting down in a draw. Thick smoke rose up from a rock chimney. The cabin was small – smaller even then Moses's cabin. There were two hogs in a fence and a mule in a lean-to barn, but no other livestock. The shutters on the cabin were all buttoned-up.

"Hello inside that cabin!" Moses Calhoun called. A dog inside began to bark. In a moment, a man with a rifle in his hand stepped out of the cabin door. He was bundled tight in a bearskin coat, and Moses couldn't see anything of the man's face because the shoulders rose up so high.

"Is that Moses Calhoun?" the man called. The voice was muffled but sounded familiar.

"It is," Moses said. "Mind if I ride in?"

"Make yourself at home," the man called back. He stepped out of the cabin and pulled the door closed to keep the heat from escaping.

Moses rode closer, and when he reached the small clearing around the cabin, he dismounted.

He saw now why he'd not recognized the man. In addition to the thick bearskin coat, he wore a beaver hide cap and a neckerchief over his face.

"Whose hospitality am I intruding upon?" Moses asked.

The man chuckled and reached up to drop his neckerchief. His face exposed, Moses saw that it was Chester Klemp.

"Well, hello, Chester," Moses said. "I did not expect to find you up here."

Chester set down his rifle and took the mule's lead

while Moses began to unsaddle his horse.

"I reckon I didn't expect to be found," Chester Klemp said.

The lean-to barn had a small paddock, and Chester opened the gate and invited Moses to put his horse in once it was unsaddled. Then Moses went to work unpacking the mule.

"What brings you up so far in such weather?" Chester Klemp asked.

"Doing a favor for an old friend," Moses said.

"Must be a good friend," Chester Klemp said. "You've come a long way from home."

After getting the pannier unstrapped and a couple of the heavier items out of it, he hefted the pack off the mule and then led it into the paddock behind the horse.

"Old Eli Simmons has a daughter with the Snake People," Moses said.

"They'll be at their winter camp, now," Chester noted.

"That's where I'm bound for," Moses said.

"Well, come inside and let's get a cup of coffee and you can tell me all about it," Chester said.

Moses laid his gear just inside the door of the cottage and stripped out of his deerskin coat to just his shirt. Chester Klemp removed his coat.

The cabin was warm with a strong fire burning in the fireplace.

"How long have you been up here?" Moses asked.

"Built this cabin last summer. Been up here just

about a year now."

Moses looked around. There was nothing special about the cabin. A simple bed. A couple of bearskin rugs. A table and a bench seat that were clearly handcrafted by Chester Klemp himself. A small table contained a dozen or so books.

Chester wasn't much of a trapper, and his skill at hunting was just sufficient to keep himself alive. He was a bit of a mystery to the other men who lived in the mountains and made their way by hunting and trapping. Most of them did what they did because they appreciated the solitude and the natural beauty of the country. They liked the mountains, they liked the rushing streams in the spring. They liked being on their own and surviving by what means they could devise themselves. They liked not being near other people. But they trapped and hunted for the money to go to town and buy provisions.

Chester Klemp preferred his books over trapping, and most of the skins he earned he kept for his own use. It was said he had come into the mountains to avoid warrants from down below.

None of that meant much to Moses Calhoun. Moses took the measure of the man he knew, not what was written about him on a piece of government paper. And Moses had found Chester Klemp to be a decent and helpful neighbor.

Chester had been in the mountains maybe five years now, and some months back he'd disappeared. He used to have a place over near Moses Calhoun's cabin, about twenty miles away. When he disappeared, Moses hoped it was a bear that got him and not the law.

Either way, Moses was relieved to find him here now.

Chester Klemp had a stew on the fire and he shared that with Calhoun, and over the meal, Klemp explained that he abandoned his previous home and came deeper into the mountains after hearing that men from the town were looking for him.

"I assumed they were lawmen," Chester said. "So I started moving until I thought I was far enough away that I wouldn't be troubled."

"You managed to get a good ways out," Calhoun said. "Indians trouble you much here?"

Chester Klemp shook his head.

"Never seen any," he said. "Bear are about all I have to worry over."

Moses glanced around at the cabin, the windows, the door. It all seemed sturdy enough to keep bear out, though he'd seen evidence over the years of bear getting into places that seemed sturdy.

The two men talked for some time, but Moses Calhoun did not reveal the details for his late-season journey other than to say he was doing a favor for Eli Simmons by going to the Snake winter camp to find Eli's daughter. In Moses's experience, it was better not to say more than was necessary, even to a trusted friend.

But he was grateful for the warmth of the cabin and a dry place to spend the night.

Dawn's light revealed a thin blanket of snow on the ground around the cabin. Under the trees, where the snow had a harder time reaching the ground, it stood in patches here and there. But the air was icy, and the gray sky from the day before remained, threatening more snow later.

"You'll make the pass without any trouble," Chester Klemp said. "This isn't enough snow to prevent travel."

Moses Calhoun grunted his doubt.

"I'll get through the pass, but when I come back in a few days it might be tougher going," he said. "That's my worry now."

"Well, you'll find a warm place to spend the night on your return if you care to stop," Chester said.

"I'm obliged," Moses said. "I might have more in my party on the way back."

Chester shrugged his shoulders.

"My garden wasn't too done under by the deer," he said. "I've stores enough, and would be glad to give a place to any who can squeeze into here."

Calhoun packed his pannier onto the mule's back and saddled his horse, and soon he was setting out for the mountain pass.

The pass was above the tree line, and Calhoun found that thin blanket of snow to be a bit thicker as he made his way out of the trees and across the alpine meadow through the saddle. But horse and mule both managed to stay sure-footed, and soon Calhoun was out the other side and descending toward the long valley where he expected to find the Snake People.

A day and a half, probably. Maybe two days.

- 8 -

Jack Cut Face rode on ahead of the soldiers to make certain the pass was clear. He had been gone for more than an hour.

"If the pass ain't clear, the regiment'll have to turn back," Bearclaw Jim predicted. "They'll have trouble enough getting their wagons up to the pass. If I was them, I'd leave the wagons and rough it from here to the Snake camp."

Lieutenant Fisher turned up his nose.

"I'm sure Colonel Culberson won't need your

advice," Fisher said.

Bearclaw Jim's pride still stung from the blow it had taken from the back of Fisher's hand.

"You'd be surprised how much Colonel Culberson listens to what I have to say," Bearclaw Jim said. "I've scouted for this army for some years now, off and on, and the colonel knows the value of my counsel, even if others under his command don't."

Fisher ignored the man.

The patrol was still making its way up through a spruce forest, making for the mountain pass when Sergeant Terry spotted a rider on the trail ahead of them.

"Halt!" he commanded the patrol, and he reached for his Colt Navy revolver. He kept five the six chambers loaded and the hammer sat on an empty chamber to prevent an accident.

"Put your saber back in its sheath, Sergeant Terry," Bearclaw Jim said. "It's just Jack Cut Face come back to report."

Terry squinted into the dark woods and saw that it was indeed their Lakota scout riding toward them.

"The pass is clear enough," Jack Cut Face said, making his report to Bearclaw Jim while the lieutenant and the sergeant listened. "Someone has passed through there this morning, though."

"What does he mean, 'passed through'?" Lieutenant Fisher demanded of Bearclaw Jim. "Who was it?"

The Lakota did not look at him; instead he continued to make his report to the old trapper.

"One man, on horseback and with a mule following," Jack Cut Face said. "He comes up from the southeast."

The soldiers were approaching the pass from the northeast.

"Is he an Indian?" Lieutenant Fisher asked.

Jack Cut Face shook his head.

"A white man," he told Bearclaw Jim.

"Is he a trapper?" the lieutenant asked.

"Only if he's a damned fool," Bearclaw Jim said. "The trappers don't come this far to the north this late in the season. They stay near to their cabins so that they don't get stranded if a blizzard blows up."

"Then what's a white man doing here?" the lieutenant asked.

Jack Cut Face gave nothing away on his face, but a slight shrug of his shoulder told Bearclaw Jim that the tracks were a mystery to the Lakota scout.

"He's no concern of ours either way," Bearclaw Jim said. "He ain't no Injun and he's just one man."

"How far ahead of us?" Sergeant Terry asked.

The Lakota scout looked at Terry. He would speak to the sergeant.

"The man rode through the pass earlier. An hour ago. Maybe two."

"Can we catch him?" Sergeant Terry asked.

"Probably," the Lakota said. "He is trailing a pack mule and will not move fast in the cold."

Sergeant Terry nodded thoughtfully, then turned his attention to his lieutenant.

"I would recommend, sir, that we make an effort to overtake and arrest the man. His presence might be enough to warn the Injuns, or at least put them on guard. He could cause trouble for us if left to wander out here on his own."

The lieutenant nodded but did not commit to a course of action.

"Let's get on the way," he said. "The longer we linger, the longer it takes us to get back to the regiment with whatever useful information we can gather."

The patrol continued on its way, riding a bit faster now. At the mountain pass, Jack Cut Face and Bearclaw Jim, along with Sergeant Terry, rode to where they could examine the tracks in the snow. They learned nothing new through their examination, but Sergeant Terry was satisfied that the man who left the tracks was traveling alone.

By midday they were through the pass and making their way back down the mountain's western face toward the valley where the scouts said they would find the Snake People.

***

Moses Calhoun made his camp under a tall lodgepole pine in a place that was sufficiently sheltered from the snow that the ground was still mostly dry.

After seeing to the horse and mule, he set about building a place for him to get through the night. As he had done on countless previous nights, he cut boughs from a couple of spruce trees to fashion himself a small shelter. His intention was to build a small fire, and in the last bit of daylight before the gloaming, Calhoun collected enough wood to cook his dinner and make coffee. But before bent to start the fire, he smelled smoke drifting in the air. It was a faint scent, but unmistakable.

When Calhoun had come across Chester Klemp's cabin the previous afternoon, it seemed inconceivable to him that there was a white man living so far into the wilderness. The smell of smoke again this afternoon was confounding. Calhoun's first thought was that the Indians must have sent a hunting party out for one last forage into the wilderness before the heavy snows came.

Calhoun gave a look around his campsite to be certain everything was secure.

The horse and mule both seemed content. As he did every night, Calhoun had tied his food to a high limb away from his shelter to keep the bears out of it. Satisfied that there was no immediate danger in the area, he took up his rifle and possibles bag with his powder horn strapped to the outside of it, and then he began to make his way through the woods, following the scent of smoke.

The smell of smoke carried him down lower, and when he came to a rocky face, he found the source.

Down in the valley, not that far below where he was camped, a group of men had built up a fire and were huddled around it.

Soldiers.

It was just a small patrol, a handful of men, but they were also evidence that the soldiers knew where to find the Snake People's winter camp and would soon be here in force.

Calhoun did not stray out onto the rock face. Instead, he stayed hidden among the trees and squatted down low, though he doubted in the dimming light the men would see him anyway. The small experience Calhoun had with soldiers was that they were not terribly observant, trusting their safety to numbers rather than to careful observation or skill.

He watched them for a moment as they went about their business. A couple of them walked away from their camp to relieve themselves. A couple of them went in among the trees close to their camp to fetch more firewood. They did not have tents with them, traveling fast and light with only blankets to keep them warm. Calhoun did not envy them the night they were going to spend in the frozen meadow. Their horses were picketed near their camp.

Twenty-six horses, Calhoun counted.

He watched the men and counted them, careful not to count any man twice who disappeared into the woods and then returned to the campsite with an armful of wood.

Twenty men, he counted. And twenty-six horses.

Calhoun let out a heavy sigh, disgusted and angry.

He stood up and made his way quietly back to his campsite.

The missing six men included an Indian scout, and a white man who had the appearance of having been in these mountains for a long time. There were also four soldiers, including one who was a sergeant. As he expected, when Calhoun returned to his campsite, he found them picking through his shelter and snooping around his campsite.

The hunter stood for a while on the edge of the small clearing around the lodgepole pine, watching the soldiers and debating what to do.

After some time, the sergeant said, "I'm tired of waiting. Cut down his food, get his horse and mule. We'll take his gear back down to our camp, and if he wants it, he can come to us to get it."

Then the sergeant held up Calhoun's bearskin coat in front of himself.

"I reckon this would keep me warm tonight," he said.

Calhoun clenched his jaw. He kept his Tennessee rifle held casually in his crossed arms so as not to present a threat, and then he stepped out from behind the spruce tree that had kept him hidden.

"No need to take any of my provisions, or my animals," Calhoun said.

Two of the privates immediately drew their heavy Colt Navy revolvers. The white scout snatched a knife from its sheath on his belt, and the Lakota reached for his own knife.

The sergeant looked around Calhoun's bearskin coat that he held out in front of him. Seeing Calhoun, he tossed it onto the ground.

"What's your name?" the sergeant demanded.

"Moses Calhoun."

"What's your business here?"

Calhoun looked around.

"I live in these mountains," he said. "It's no strange thing for me to be here."

He put them emphasis on himself, implying that it was strange for the soldiers to be here.

"Are you alone?" the sergeant asked.

"Not now," Calhoun said, gesturing to the sergeant and the soldiers around him. "But I was before you turned up in my campsite, riffling through my belongings and tossing them on the ground."

"You ain't close to home up here," the older scout said. He still had his hand on the grip of his knife, but he had returned it to its sheath and seemed to have relaxed a little.

"I'm a sight closer than you are," Calhoun said.

"You're not hunting," the old scout said. "What are you doing?"

"Traveling," Calhoun said.

The old scout sniffed and squinted doubtfully.

"I think you'd best come with us," the sergeant said.

The privates with their guns stiffened a bit, as if ready to meet a fight.

"I appreciate the offer, but I can make my own way," Calhoun said.

The sergeant chuckled.

"It's not an offer, Mr. Calhoun. My name is Sergeant Terry, and I'm afraid we'll be taking you as a prisoner. Private Chandler, disarm the prisoner."

One of the privates holstered his gun and took a step toward Calhoun. When the mountain hunter turned his gaze on the private, the man froze in his tracks. Hep Chandler saw in the mountain hunter's eyes a fire that unmanned him.

"Go on," the sergeant said. "Take his gun and that hatchet and any other weapons he has."

The hatchet hung loosely at Calhoun's thigh in a

looped cord tied to his belt. His big Bowie knife was in a sheath on his belt at the small of his back.

The private took a tentative step forward, and seeing that Calhoun wasn't going to put up a fight, he now stepped hurriedly over to Calhoun. He took the rifle. He slid the hatchet from its looped cord. He took the knife from its sheath. He searched the possibles bag.

"Pack up your gear, Calhoun."

"Why am I being taken prisoner?"

"We're arresting you as a traitor," Sergeant Terry said. "I hear that twang in your voice, and I reckon you're a Southern man. We'll let the colonel decide whether or not to put you on trial."

Calhoun did not move. Of course he knew of the war back east. His native North Carolina had seceded, and he knew that, too. But none of that was anything to him. In the mountains, there was no country, no government, no loyalty, no secession. All that existed in this place was survival.

"I've not taken up arms against anyone or any government," Calhoun said. "You've got no cause to arrest me."

The sergeant shrugged, indifferent.

"The colonel can decide that when we get to him."

Calhoun chewed his lip, but he reasoned that it would be unwise to try to make a stand. He might be able to fight off two or three of the soldiers, maybe all four of them. But the Indian scout, who looked to be a Lakota, was too cool, and Calhoun knew he would fight like venom. Also, Calhoun expected these men would be unwittingly taking him to his intended destination.

Though he did regret losing his shelter for the night and was not looking forward to spending the night in the frozen meadow with the soldiers.

- 9 -

Even with his coat and blanket and the fire crackling nearby, Moses Calhoun spent a miserable night in the cold. The meadow was wet with snow. But he made no complaint. In fact, he did not say much of anything.

A man who called himself Lieutenant Fisher questioned Calhoun at length, but Moses revealed nothing of his purpose in the mountains, saying only that he was traveling before winter set in. Calhoun noted that the man's breath smelled of cheap whiskey and his eyes were bloodshot.

The older scout attempted to make conversation, but Calhoun would not respond to him. He named off men he knew in the area, trappers and hunters who had been here a long time. Calhoun knew all of the names. He'd met all of the men at one time or another. He also knew they had all been here for many years, suggesting that this scout had left the area some time ago. He mentioned Eli Simmons as one he had known, but Calhoun did not give any indication that he knew Simmons better than any of the others named.

The old scout asked questions about the beaver and the buffalo.

"Beaver was gettin' thin when I was last trapping in this area," he said. "Are they more plentiful now?"

"How are the buffalo herds?"

"See many grizz about?"

The old scout peppered him with these questions, but Calhoun either ignored them or grunted noncommittal answers. At last Bearclaw Jim lost his patience with the man.

"I think you're up in these mountains for no good," Bearclaw Jim said, a sting in his tone. "If I had to guess, I'd say you've come all this way to talk to the Injuns. Maybe you know the army is coming. Maybe you've come to warn them. If it was up to me, I reckon I'd put a knife in your gut and spill your innards and leave you for the wolves to eat."

Moses Calhoun didn't rise to the threat, though he also did not doubt that Bearclaw Jim would do it if given provocation or permission.

Being taken prisoner, for now, was nothing more than an inconvenience. Calhoun suspected that when he was ready, he would find that getting free would prove to be an easy enough chore.

The troopers took turns watching him through the night. They bound his wrists together to keep him from trying to make an escape.

In the morning, they untied him so that he could pack his mule and saddle his horse.

Other than taking his weapons, they left his provisions alone and made no effort to harass or harm him. He was allowed to cook his own breakfast and coffee on their fire, and no one objected to the little things he did to try to provide himself with some comfort, whether it was standing by the fire or going through his gear for a change of socks.

Moses Calhoun understood what was going on, though none of the soldiers let on.

They had taken him prisoner to keep him from unwittingly alerting the Snake People to the presence of the soldiers. This patrol intended to reconnoiter the Snake tribe's winter camp. The threat, as the soldiers saw it, was that Moses would see them and report to the Snake people that he'd seen soldiers in the area. So he had been arrested. If the soldiers kept him as a prisoner until such time that they were prepared to make an attack, he couldn't foul up their plans.

Of course they did not know that his intention was to do just that, and they probably did not know that he was aware that the entire regiment was somewhere behind them.

So Moses Calhoun played the role of the hopeless prisoner.

He rode along in the center of their line, pulling his

mule to keep up with the soldiers. He did as he was told, and he made no move to escape.

The older scout, who called himself Bearclaw Jim, gave up trying to make friends.

The Lakota scout, who never made an effort to make friends, often rode far ahead of the soldiers, out of sight.

When he was around, he eyed Moses Calhoun suspiciously. He seemed to understand what the soldiers did not – that Moses Calhoun's presence in the mountains was something more than he let on. Of course the Lakota would have recognized the bead work on Calhoun's hatchet, and he would know that Moses had a relationship of some kind with the Snake people. The hatchet had been a gift, given to him by Chief Mukuakantun. The beads tied into the leather wrapping would have been obvious to a Lakota.

A light snow started mid-morning. It was nothing like the snow of the previous day with the big heavy flakes, and it fell intermittently through the late morning and afternoon, and what fell from the sky stuck to the ground, deepening the snow in the valley meadow.

Later in the afternoon, but still well before dusk, the Lakota came into view riding toward them.

The old scout, the lieutenant, and the sergeant rode out ahead to meet him.

There was discussion that Calhoun did not hear, and when the four of them returned to the main body of the patrol, they ordered the men to make camp at the edge of a forest that crept down into the meadow not far from where the men were currently sitting their horses.

Moses Calhoun understood.

The Lakota scout had gone ahead and discovered the Snake People's camp. They were close enough now that they did not want to get any closer for fear of being discovered.

Calhoun didn't say anything as he unpacked his mule, but he listened close to the conversations among the men. Neither the lieutenant nor the sergeant were letting on to the others why they were stopping so early in the day and giving up daylight that could have been used to keep riding. The men, though, had no qualms about discussing their theories in front of Calhoun.

Ultimately, the troopers seemed to reach the consensus that they must be approaching the winter camp of the Snake tribe.

With the lieutenant and the sergeant now standing some distance from the men and consulting with the two scouts, Calhoun took the opportunity to question some of the troopers who were talking.

"Why do you men care where the Snake tribe is camped?" Calhoun asked.

"We're going up to their camp to have a look around," one of the younger troopers said.

"What for?"

Another of the troopers, whose name Calhoun had learned was Hep Chandler, chuckled a little.

"Because them's our orders, and in the cavalry, a man does what he's told."

"I reckon so," Calhoun said. "That winter camp is going to be full of warriors. Surely twenty-four troopers, two scouts, and one prisoner aren't expected to engage them?"

The younger trooper said, "We're just observing. If an attack is going to be made, the regiment coming up behind us will do it. They have warrants for some of the men in the camp."

"Hush, Chris," Hep Chandler said. "This man don't need to know all that."

"Chris?" Calhoun said. "I had a cousin back home named Christopher. He and I used to go around a good bit together. Fishing, hunting deer in the mountains."

"He a Reb, too?" another of the soldiers asked.

"I ain't a Rebel," Moses Calhoun said. "As for my cousin, he ain't neither. Some years ago, before I left home, he got caught in a river undertow and drowned."

The soldier lowered his eyes and nodded his head. A small apology for speaking of the dead.

"No, boys, I ain't no Rebel," Calhoun said. "I reckon plenty of my people back in North Carolina are fighting, but I left the fights of other men back East when I come out here. The only man I fight for now is myself, and sometimes my neighbor."

"We're trying to get to the war, but the War Department has other ideas," Hep Chandler said.

"Other ideas about attacking the Indians?" Calhoun asked.

Chandler chuckled.

"Hell, the War Department don't even know we're doing it. Not yet. They'll find out when it's done. Them Indians killed too many white folks."

"You sure you got the right Indians?" Calhoun asked.

"One Indian ain't no different from another," another

private said. He and the one they called Chris were the youngest of the troopers.

"What's your name, son?" Calhoun asked.

"Billy Douglas."

"Well, Billy, you see that old scout y'all have with you?" Calhoun asked, nodding to where the officer was talking to the scouts.

"Sure."

"Is he anything like you?" Moses Calhoun asked.

The soldiers had all turned their noses up at Bearclaw Jim more times than a few. He was foul smelling, foul mouthed, and he had a foul attitude. His jokes were crass and usually at the expense of the younger soldiers.

"No, he ain't nothin' like me," Billy Douglas confessed.

"And do you think you and I are anything alike?" Calhoun asked.

Billy gave him an appraising look, and finally shook his head.

"I reckon not. Not much, anyway."

Calhoun nodded.

"That's right. We're three very different men," Calhoun said. "And you wouldn't want to be held responsible for my crimes, or I for Mr. Bearclaw's crimes."

"Hogwash," Hep Chandler said. "Injuns is Injuns, and that's that."

Calhoun nodded. He knew the attitude of most of the

whites, settlers and soldiers alike. At best, the Indians were a nuisance to be pushed off valuable land. And the Indians had done their share to exacerbate the hostilities, some through theft but others through terrible massacres of defenseless settlers.

What distinguished Calhoun from the others wasn't his acceptance of the atrocities, but his friendship with some among the tribes. Though he suspected, too, that some he called "friend" were guilty of murdering white settlers, and he knew that some had raided settlements and stolen livestock.

The soldiers made their fire and cooked their dinner. They did not offer to share with Moses Calhoun, but they allowed him his freedom to cook his own dinner from his own provisions.

When his supper was done and his blanket laid out, the soldiers bound Calhoun's wrists again. They left his hands in front of him to give him some ability to arrange his blanket or get at his provisions. Then all except one of the soldiers walked away from the camp where the lieutenant began issuing orders. Calhoun could hear him talking, and sometimes one or another of the soldiers would ask a question. Though he could hear the voices, he could not make out what they were saying.

***

Lieutenant Fisher gathered the men together away from the campsite, leaving Chris Dolan with a cocked Colt Navy to stand guard over the prisoner.

"The winter camp is about five miles beyond our present position," Lieutenant Fisher said. "I'm leaving four men here to guard the prisoner, and the rest of us are going to use the cover of night to make our way to the encampment. Our scout, Jack Cut Face, says they are camped at the base of a mesa, and a forest along the sides of that prominence will give us an opportunity to get near to the camp and observe it without being seen."

"Who will stay with the prisoner?" Sergeant Terry asked, hopeful – though doubtful – this duty would fall to him. Sergeant Terry didn't care for Lieutenant Fisher's aptitude as a military officer. It was fine around the fort or on patrol when no threat existed, but in a bad situation, Sergeant Terry did not want to be in a position to have to take orders from Lieutenant Fisher. The thought had crossed his mind before that if he ever found himself following Fisher into battle, he'd shoot the man himself before following his lead.

The lieutenant looked at Craig Dolan, brother of the young private already guarding the prisoner.

"Dolan, Chandler and Douglas," Lieutenant Fisher said. "The three of you, along with young Dolan back there, will stay with the prisoner, the horses, and our spare gear."

Sergeant Terry grunted his disappointment, but he wasn't the only one disappointed by the order. The three men who were told they would stay behind weren't happy about it, either.

All of the boys in the patrol, just like those back with the regiment, joined up because they wanted to fight Rebels, and in lieu of Southern traitors, they'd accept Indian fighting. But nobody – other than Sergeant Terry – wanted to be left behind to guard a man who, by all appearances, was loyal to neither the Southerners nor the Indians.

"Lieutenant, why don't we just turn the prisoner loose so that we can all go?" Hep Chandler asked.

"You'll get your chance at them Injuns, don't you fret, Private Chandler," Lieutenant Fisher said, smiling at his favorite.

He ignored the other complaints coming from the three men who had been told that they would stay behind to guard the prisoner and addressed those men who were going with the patrol.

"We'll move into position tonight under cover of darkness," Fisher said. "We'll take up positions on the ridge overlooking the camp, and through the day tomorrow we will all stay secluded. If we allow ourselves to be seen, it'll be a disaster for our campaign. So once you're in a spot tonight, you don't move."

Fisher went through his 20-man roster, designating specific duties.

Some of the men were to count warriors – obvious men of fighting age in the camp. Others were to count teepees. Fisher knew that they wouldn't get a precisely accurate count, but what he needed was a general estimate of the Indians' numbers in their winter camp that he could take back to Colonel Culberson. Others were to do what they could to determine what sort of arms the Indians might have.

He designated a couple of men to watch for patrols or guards so that they could provide an idea of how the Indians were protecting their camp.

"Sergeant Terry and I will make a judgment on the best routes for attack," Fisher said, and Sergeant Terry understood that to mean that he would make a judgment on the best routes for attack because Lieutenant Fisher would be drinking from his flask and unable to make a clear-headed determination.

"The most important thing is that we make our observations without being observed ourselves," Fisher said again. "We're here to assist the regiment in its planning, not to give away the impending attack."

Sergeant Terry muttered something to the lieutenant, and Fisher nodded.

"Men, whether you are going forward or staying here to guard the prisoner, cap your revolvers," the lieutenant said. "Be very careful that there are no accidental discharges that might alert the Indians. But we're in hostile territory now, and we should be armed accordingly."

With his orders issued, Lieutenant Fisher dismissed his men until dark.

The men came back into the camp to gather the gear they intended to take with them. The three who were being left behind with Chris Dolan explained the situation to him while he stood guard over Moses Calhoun, and through their explanation they told Calhoun all he needed to know as if he had been with them when they received their orders from Lieutenant Fisher.

Calhoun watched the men as they gathered the supplies they would take.

Each man in the outfit was armed with two Colt Navy revolvers and a cavalry saber. They left those sabers, now, each man taking only his brace of revolvers. The lieutenant and the sergeant each had field glasses. The men took pouches with extra ammunition and percussion caps for their guns. They took canteens, and a couple of them were smart enough to take some jerky for the day-long mission. All the rest of their gear they left behind.

In the remnants of the dusk, the men set out on foot with the two scouts leading the way.

- 10 -

Moses Calhoun sat with his back against a large lodgepole pine. He'd piled up pine straw in an effort to give himself a dry seat, and he'd pulled his blanket up over his body, tucking it around him.

The four soldiers left behind to guard him sat around the fire, paying little attention to their prisoner.

Calhoun watched the men with interest. They were all so young, younger than he was when he first came into the mountains to trap and hunt for pelts.

They huddled around the fire, using a fallen pine

tree for a bench. Each man had on his heavy wool coat with his blanket draped over his shoulders, and still they shivered against the cold night. They tried to make each other feel better about being left behind.

"Them others is going to freeze tonight," Hep Chandler said. "Not a man amongst 'em took a blanket."

"They'll walk half the night and freeze the other half," Craig Dolan agreed. "Army life ain't about comfort, I suppose."

"Hell, I ain't comfortable now," Hep Chandler said. "And we've got fire and blankets, and we ain't walking five miles."

"I'd still rather be with them than sitting here watching the horses," Chris Dolan said.

With the blanket covering his body, Moses Calhoun propped his knees up and dropped his hands down between his knees. There, where no one could see his movements, his fingers went to work on the knot binding his wrists. He'd given the soldiers no cause to give him a thought. Even now they ignored their prisoner. And because he'd been so accommodating, they'd been careless in binding his wrists. His hands tied to the front gave him mobility he'd have not had if they had tied his hands behind his back. They'd failed to pull the knot as tight as possible. If they were serious about their work, they'd have tied his arms to the tree to keep him from having any hope of gaining his freedom.

But instead, they'd treated him as an afterthought.

By shifting his wrists back and forth, Calhoun was able to work some slack into the rope around his wrists. Then it was simply an issue of patience – patiently working a loose end of the rope back through the knot. It would have been easier if he could have seen what he was doing, but his fingers felt the knot, and slowly he began to set himself free.

While he worked, he listened to the idle ramble of the four boys left to guard him.

"What will we do with the prisoners when we attack the camp?" Billy Douglas said.

"There won't be prisoners," Hep Chandler answered him. "We'll rout that camp, and the only ones who survive will be the ones who flee into the hills. And them, we'll let go."

"What about the womenfolk? And the children?" Billy Douglas asked. "Won't there be women and children at the camp?"

"Injun women just make more Injun thieves and murderers," Hep Chandler said. "And the children just grow up to be thieves and murderers. When we go to attack that camp, what you've got to remember is the white folks they've been killing and stealing from. You don't think about them being women and children. You just think about the terrible torture and murder they've committed."

Calhoun leaned his head back against the tree and shut his eyes. He felt the rope give way, and now his hands were free.

He did not relish the thought of killing these four soldiers, though he did not doubt that he had the ability to do it. These four boys were young and strong enough, and they probably would be hell in a fair fight. But Moses Calhoun had lived a long time in a hostile world. He'd wrestled mountain lions and killed two bears with nothing more than his hands and knife. He'd fought

Indians and white men, alike, and often at a numerical disadvantage. But all of those fights had been fights for his life. This was different. These men weren't going to kill him, and Moses did not want to kill them, either.

Instead, he decided he should wait. At some point a couple of them would bed-down. They'd probably take turns on watch, two at a time. If two of them fell asleep, he'd have a better chance of not having to kill any of them. The trick, probably, would be to lay hands on their guns. They would likely be more compliant if they were facing a brace of cocked revolvers.

And so he did not stir. He kept his head back against the tree, his eyes shut. And he waited.

They talked late into the night and kept feeding their fire, until at last one of them – Craig Dolan – said, "A couple of us had better bed down. Chris and Billy, you take the first watch. Hep and I will sleep for a couple of hours, and then you wake us up and we'll take the watch."

There was general agreement to this, and Calhoun listened as the men by the campfire broke up.

He cracked his eyes enough to watch one of the men walk down to where the horses were tied. Two of them made themselves pallets of pine straw and stretched out near the fire.

The fourth man, Billy Douglas, took a turn around the campsite, staying within the circle of light cast by the fire. He made a complaint about his toes being frozen, and one of the men laying down said his entire body felt like it would never thaw.

Moses Calhoun waited.

With his eyelids barely raised, he watched Chris

Dolan walk back up from the horses to take a seat on the log by the fire. Billy Douglas stomped his feet to shake off the cold, and one of the men lying down told him to keep quiet. Douglas came back and sat beside the younger Dolan boy and pulled his blanket back up over his shoulders.

Moses Calhoun watched them.

Had it been summer or early fall, all four of those soldiers would likely have already been scalped and their carcasses strewn over the campsite for the birds and wolves to fight over. Their fire was burning for warmth and light, without any consideration for how it might attract their enemies. Their watch consisted of looking into the flames in the fire pit. A thousand Snake warriors could be creeping just outside their campsite, and these four men would have never known it. They were hapless fools, inexperienced and ill trained.

Slowly, over half an hour or so, Calhoun could hear the two men stretched under their blankets drift to sleep. Their breathing relaxed and leveled out.

His own weapons were with the saddles and other gear. The hatchet, particularly, was a prized possession for Moses Calhoun, but his Tennessee rifle was the difference between life and starvation, and so he had kept his eyes on his weapons and knew exactly where they were. But before he could get to his weapons he would have to deal with the soldiers. He was confident he could disarm the two keeping watch before the others were roused by the commotion, but he would have to act quickly.

The log they sat on was about a dozen yards away, and the fire burned between Calhoun and the two soldiers. They would see any movement he made, but his one advantage was that neither man held a gun in his hand. Both of them had their Navy revolvers holstered at their sides.

As he was contemplating how he would attack them, Calhoun experienced a stroke of luck.

Somewhere in the woods, not terribly far away, a screech owl let out a high-pitched screech and went crashing through the woods.

The noise was tremendous enough that both men jumped from their bench and looked behind them.

Moses Calhoun moved quickly, taking advantage of their sudden fright.

He stood, shaking off the wool blanket, and let his heavy bearskin coat fall off of him as he took a couple of silent steps forward.

His movement caught the attention of one of the soldiers, but Calhoun moved quickly. He swung a fist that collided with the side of the man's head, stunning him. Then Calhoun fell on the other one, wrapping an arm around the man's throat from behind and cutting off his air.

It was Billy Douglas he'd punched, and Billy was on all fours on the ground, his head swimming. It was Chris Dolan he had in a headlock. Dolan at first grasped at Calhoun's arms, trying to get a grip, but Calhoun twisted himself and squeezed his arm tighter. Dolan made for his gun, but couldn't draw it in time. Calhoun felt the boy's body go limp in his grip as he passed out from lack of air.

He dropped Chris Dolan to the ground and then turned his attention back to Billy Douglas. He flipped the young soldier onto his back and landed another hard punch in the side of his head.

Douglas was dazed, if not completely unconscious. The tussle had made a bit of noise, but neither of the sleeping soldiers stirred. Both had pulled their wool blankets over their heads and were fast asleep.

Calhoun stripped both soldiers of their gunbelts.

He bound their wrists behind their backs and laid them both out near the fire. Both Hep Chandler and Craig Dolan had already done him the service of removing their own gunbelts while they slept, so Moses Calhoun picked those up and set them away from the camp with the other gear left by the soldiers gone out on foot patrol.

Then he stood over Hep Chandler's cocooned body and gently prodded him awake with a foot.

Chandler mumbled something grumpily, and Calhoun prodded him again.

Now Hep Chandler pulled the blanket down from his face, and Calhoun pressed the cold steel barrel of Billy Douglas's Colt Navy against his forehead.

In a whisper, Calhoun said, "I'd rather not have to shoot you. Put your hands out of the blanket where I can see them."

Chandler let out a heavy sigh, knowing this wasn't going to go well with the lieutenant.

He stuck his hands feebly out of the blanket.

"Stand up, slowly and quietly," Calhoun told him. "Turn and face the fire."

With Chandler standing away from him, Calhoun slid the Navy revolver into his waistband. He took some string he'd found and bound the man's wrists behind his back. He did it quickly, tying the knot firmly as he had on the other two. Chris Dolan was starting to stir, and

Calhoun wanted to get his brother under control before he woke up.

"Now have a seat beside the other two," Calhoun whispered at Chandler.

He repeated the process with the older Dolan boy, and when Craig's wrists were bound and all four soldiers were seated by the fire, Moses Calhoun covered them in their blankets, tucking the blankets in around the shoulders.

"What do you intend to do with us?" Craig Dolan asked.

"Leave you here," Calhoun said. "I've appreciated your hospitality, but I have important business to tend to. I'm a long way from home, and if you men delay me further, I'll have hell getting home before the heavy snow starts. I hate to leave you like this, but you'll be warm enough to make it through the day until the rest of your outfit shows back up."

Calhoun gave Chris Dolan a couple of gentle slaps on the face to rouse the boy. Then he checked on Billy Douglas.

"Can you hear me, Private Douglas?" Calhoun asked him.

Billy Douglas had a swollen eye and an angry look.

"You wouldn't have got away with that if my back hadn't been turned," Billy Douglas said.

"No, I reckon you're right about that," Moses Calhoun said. "I'm right grateful to that old screech owl that got you to turn your back on me."

Calhoun retrieved his long rifle, hatchet and Bowie knife from the gear that was stowed in the campsite. He gathered up his other belongings and stacked them nearby, then he went down and found his horse and mule and took them out from the cavalry's horses.

It took him some time to get the pannier on the mule and his saddle on his horse. He kept having to pull his leather gloves off to buckle or cinch a strap, and the cold seemed to instantly cut through his hands and freeze his fingers.

With his gear packed and his horse and mule ready, Calhoun took the time to check the ropes on the soldiers. He cinched them tight, securing them one last time. He knew they would get out of the ropes. Once he was gone, they would be able to work together, two men back-to-back, and untie the ropes. But it would take them some time, and he would be well away.

"Good luck in you campaigning, boys," Calhoun told them. "Please offer my thanks to your lieutenant for his courtesy, and my apologies that I cannot remain with your party. But my responsibilities to my family preclude me staying longer with you."

***

Calhoun deliberately led the horse and mule down into the meadow and turned east, away from the Snake People's winter camp. He chose to walk the horse rather than ride, even though the snow glowed white in the moonlight and would have made riding possible. But if his horse stepped in a hole and dumped him or turned its leg and went lame, it could prove to be a disaster for him. If they caught him, the soldiers would probably shoot him for escaping. At the very least, they would have a legitimate charge against him, and he might find himself all the way back at their fort standing trial. If that happened, his promise to Eli Simmons would be broken, and more importantly, his promise to return home to help his family through the winter would also be broken.

So he walked through what remained of the night, his feet freezing as he plodded through the thin layer of snow on the valley floor.

Neither the horse nor mule were much in the mood for walking through the night. Calhoun had the mule tied to the horse's saddle horn, but several times he had to take the mule's lead rope and give it a heavy tug to keep the animal moving in the cold night.

At dawn, Calhoun mounted the sorrel horse and rode. He estimated he'd probably walked six miles in the dark hours of morning, and he made another several miles riding through the morning light. In the distance he could see the mountain pass he had crossed through on the way to the winter camp. Calhoun's plan was to return to within a few miles of where the soldiers had first taken him prisoner. When he was satisfied that he was close enough, he would turn north and ride into the forest and there, where his tracks would be more difficult to follow, he would back-track to the Snake People's winter camp.

No fresh snow fell during the day, but the clouds remained and there was no sun to melt off the snow in the meadow. Unless the night brought a heavy snow, Calhoun knew his tracks would be visible to the soldiers.

After cutting north into the woods, he started back west, following the meadow but staying out of sight. In the woods, he again was on his feet, walking with the horse and mule trailing him. He was careful to avoid snow patches where he could, hopeful that neither the old man Bearclaw Jim nor the Lakota Jack Cut Face would wander into the woods and search for his trail. A good tracker would find him, if they were so committed.

He risked a small fire when he camped that night.

Though he had tied leather thongs around the tops of his boots, the snow and water still had a way of making it in through the tops, and he needed to dry his socks, his boots, and his feet.

He dug a hole and made the fire down in the hole so that the light would not be seen, though he suspected that was more than was necessary. He'd watched the meadow as he made his way through the woods, and he was more careful than he had been about his surroundings.

Calhoun was certain no one was around when he made his camp that night.

Whatever else he saw the next day, he now intended to ride directly into the Snake camp the next day. He estimated he was not more than fifteen miles away, now. If the soldiers were still watching the winter camp, he would worry about that later.

Moses Calhoun had been in this valley in warmer seasons when it was full of green. Now, even the boughs of the spruce and the needles of the lodgepole pines seemed gray like the sky. Nothing felt warm or alive here, and it struck him how dramatically everything could change in a short time.

In the coming days, this gray and cold place would be much worse than gray and cold. In a few days, this valley would be a place of death.

- 11 -

By morning the soldiers had worked themselves free of the cords Moses Calhoun had used to bind their wrists.

"I feel like a dern fool," Craig Dolan said.

"How'd you let him jump you?" Hep Chandler demanded of Chris Dolan and Billy Douglas.

"He just jumped us," Billy Douglas said. "He was like a mountain lion the way he sprang on us. He hit me and I was done."

"He choked me," Chris Dolan said. "I thought he was going to kill me."

"When the lieutenant gets back, we'll all wish he killed us," Craig Dolan said miserably. Court martial. That phrase ran through his head over and over again.

"It wasn't our fault," Billy Douglas said.

"That don't matter," Hep Chandler told him. "The prisoner was in our custody, and he got away. That's the only thing that matters."

"Should we go after him?" Chris Dolan asked.

Hep Chandler grunted a laugh.

"And get killed," he said. "Did you see that coat he was wearing? That was a bearskin coat, and I can guarantee you he didn't buy that in no store down in a town. He shot that bear with that long rifle. And if he can shoot a bear and make a coat out of him, what do you think he'll do to you?"

Craig Dolan shook his head in disgust listening to the others talk.

"We're going to spend the rest of the war in the fort's stockade. We thought it was bad before, the next five years of our lives are going to be misery."

Hep Chandler looked up at the gray clouds of the morning.

"I reckon so."

The men had plenty of time to contemplate their fate.

The lieutenant and the rest of the patrol remained at their observations throughout the day, watching the comings and goings at the crowded Indian camp.

Lieutenant Fisher and Sergeant Terry noted the natural defenses of the winter camp.

To the south and west, the winter camp was protected by large mesas that would prevent any kind of attack from those directions. To the northwest, there was a large forest of spruce and pine. Not impenetrable, but certainly difficult for a large body of men to move through in organized fashion. To the east – the direction from which the regiment would come unless it moved to flank the camp – was the wide-open meadow and a wide but shallow river. Crossing the river would not be difficult. The regiment could make an open charge across the river and be immediately in the Snake Indians' camp. But the meadow presented more of a problem. Unless the regiment was to skirt the edge of the forest to the north, the open meadow would allow the Indians too much warning because they would see the regiment riding to them. The meadow was almost completely flat.

The Snake camp was spread out over several acres. Livestock consisted of some horses and cattle, but not many of either. The cattle were stolen from settlers and travelers killed on the trail, and most of the horses likely were, too. Lieutenant Fisher noted the animals as evidence that the impending attack against the winter camp would be justified.

"A dawn attack would work," Sergeant Terry suggested. "We can use the cover of darkness to get the men in position, and make the charge at dawn."

Lieutenant Fisher nodded agreement.

"It's almost the only way," he said.

The other men counted teepees or warriors, whatever was their assignment. Their estimates put the Snake population at close to two thousand with perhaps as many as eight hundred or a thousand warriors. It was hard to say. From their position on the hill overlooking the camp, it was sometimes difficult to judge if a boy was old enough to also be a potential warrior or if a man was too old to put up much of a fight. The Indians were all so bundled against the cold, that Sergeant Terry was certain some women and some feeble old men and some young boys managed to get counted among the warriors. The sergeant, who was the most experienced military man in the outfit, estimated the strength of the Snake warriors to come to around four hundred – which would put them at almost an even draw with the four companies of the regiment currently moving through the valley behind them to attack the winter camp.

But Sergeant Terry knew the attack would never be a draw.

The Snake People were armed with a patchwork of broken and outdated weapons. Mostly they got their arms from fur traders or settlers who traded old and often broken guns. In some cases they got good rifles from skirmishes with settlers. But mostly the Snake warriors carried old smoothbore muskets. There were very few rifles, and they were inaccurate with those.

Sergeant Terry did note locations around the camp where the Snake people dug rifle pits and thatched spruce branches to make blinds that would hide their numbers and give them shelter in defense of an attack, but for the most part they seemed to be relying on the natural defenses of their position – the difficulty of approach to the winter camp.

"It's a shame we cannot employ canon," Lieutenant Fisher said.

Sergeant Terry agreed with his lieutenant, though he doubted that canon would have much impact on the outcome of the engagement. Everything Sergeant Terry saw suggested to him that the result was a foregone conclusion. There would be a slaughter at the winter camp.

Late in the afternoon, a small group of Snake men rode out from the camp, crossing the river. Sergeant Terry took special interest in watching the men cross the river. Simply observing the river, Terry had deemed it to be wide but not deep. Now he was able to get confirmation. It did not reach much above the knees of the horses. He pointed this out to his lieutenant.

"Best approach to attack the camp will be to come into the meadow and make a dawn charge right across the river," Terry said. "We can send a detachment north to cross the river downstream, out of sight, and circle in behind to make a flanking approach. That would cut off any line of retreat."

The lieutenant nodded agreement.

***

After sunset, the soldiers abandoned their observations from the cover of trees on the mesa overlooking the winter camp, and they made their way through the trees away from the camp.

They had a walk of about five miles to return to the campsite where they left their horses and the four-man guard with the prisoner.

Lieutenant Fisher and Sergeant Terry had both been moderately concerned about the party that left the winter camp late in the afternoon but never returned.

"It's just a hunting party," Bearclaw Jim told them.

Nevertheless, they'd kept the men together during their return hike through the meadow, and they'd quickly silenced any unnecessary chatter.

Sergeant Terry was already disgusted when he walked into camp because the Dolan brothers and the two others had built up a campfire that could be seen through the tree branches from the meadow. Adding to his anger, of course, the sergeant and the other men had spent a freezing day and night in observation of the winter camp, and his feet were near frozen from the walk back to camp. A cavalryman's boots were not made to walk so much, and particularly not through the snow.

"Why is this fire so high?" Sergeant Terry demanded.

"We just wanted to give you a nice, warm home to come back to," Hep Chandler said.

"You want to announce to every Injun in these mountains that you're camped here?" Sergeant Terry asked.

Chandler, seeing the sergeant's foul mood, decided not to answer.

Craig Dolan stepped up to Lieutenant Fisher. He'd tried to convince Hep Chandler to do it because Hep was one of the lieutenant's favorites, but Hep declined. Craig, being the older brother, had always been the most responsible of their group.

"Lieutenant, I need to make a report," Craig Dolan said.

Webb Fisher waved him off.

"Not right now," he said. "I'm half froze and starving."

"I should say it sooner rather than later, sir," Dolan

said. "It's about the prisoner, sir."

"What is it?" Fisher said, aggravated that the private was delaying his getting to the fire. Lieutenant Fisher, for his part, was pleased to see the fire burning so well.

"The prisoner escaped last night."

Fisher's face flashed hot, and he turned first to Sergeant Terry. Then he looked back to Craig Dolan.

"What happened?" he asked. "How did he get away?"

Billy Douglas and Chris Dolan were standing nearby, there to accept their responsibility in the escape.

"Private Chandler and I were asleep," Craig Dolan said. "Private Douglas and Private Dolan, my brother, were watching him. They were distracted by something in the woods, and the prisoner jumped them."

"He was bound when we left here," Sergeant Terry said. "Did you untie him?"

Dolan shook his head.

"No, sir. He untied himself without our knowledge."

The lieutenant and the sergeant both looked at each other.

Bearclaw Jim was also standing nearby.

"He's gone to warn the Injuns," Bearclaw Jim said. "We should have killed him when we had the chance."

Lieutenant Fisher did not give up on the conversation, but he stepped closer to the fire.

"How long has he been gone?" Fisher asked.

"He broke loose sometime before sunup," Dolan said.

"So gone all day," Fisher said, glancing at Bearclaw

Jim.

"Plenty of time to make a fair distance," Jim said.

"But he did not go to the Indian encampment," Fisher said. "We'd have seen him ride in."

"Unless he come in from the back," Bearclaw Jim said. "Could have crossed that river downstream, come into the camp from the north under the cover of the forest beyond the camp."

Fisher shook his head.

"I still believe we would have seen. We observed the camp throughout the day."

Bearclaw Jim shrugged dismissively.

"What do you think, Sergeant Terry?"

Terry, who was grateful for the warmth of the fire but would not say it, shrugged his shoulders.

"Hard to say, Lieutenant," Terry said. "I think these boys have earned themselves a court martial."

Fisher nodded.

"If it turns out that man did go to the Indians, and if that can be proved, we've all earned a court martial. The four of them, and you and me, too."

Bearclaw Jim grinned at the thought. He'd gladly testify at a court martial that he had tried to warn Fisher that the prisoner presented a danger to the expedition and advised to execute the man. Bearclaw Jim felt no loyalty to Lieutenant Webb Fisher, and anything he could do to raise his own estimation among the army's other officers would only improve his opportunity of being hired on with the army in the future.

Lieutenant Webb Fisher didn't grin.

He took a heavy sigh and snatched his hat from his head so that he could rub his forehead with the ball of his gloved-hand.

"He took one of my six-shooters, too," Chris Dolan said, feeling that the bad news should all be given at once.

"Well, damnation, son!" Lieutenant Fisher shouted. "I reckon it would be your good luck if he shot and killed you with it, too."

Chris Dolan dropped his eyes.

Lieutenant Fisher replaced his hat and grabbed Bearclaw Jim by the arm.

"Tell me now. Can you track this man?"

Bearclaw Jim hemmed and hawed for a moment. He mumbled something about the snowfall and losing the tracks among the trees. He said something about how the man might be anywhere by now. But then, finally, he nodded his head toward Jack Cut Face.

"That man there could track him, I reckon," Bearclaw Jim said. "He could track him all the way to Washington D.C., I reckon."

"Fine then," Lieutenant Fisher said. "Sergeant, at first light we move out to track down our prisoner."

Most of the men had pushed in to be close to the fire, or as close as they could get, and as a result they had been privy to the entire conversation. They knew that the prisoner had escaped, and they knew that rather than returned directly to the remainder of the regiment riding up from the fort, they would be detoured to go in search of the escaped prisoner.

Returning to the regiment would not have eased their cold and discomfort. The mountain trails through the pine and spruce forests and the rocky inclines of the passes precluded wagons or caissons. There was no artillery riding in support of the cavalry. So returning to the rest of the regiment would not have meant tents or cots or other comforts. But in their minds, they had looked forward to returning to the regiment with the belief that they would somehow be less miserable.

Now, it seemed, the escaped prisoner was costing them a longer duration of misery.

The general grousing around the campfire that followed the lieutenant's announcement was all directed toward the two Dolan brothers, Hep Chandler and young Bill Douglas, whose eye was now black and swollen.

"You heard the lieutenant," Sergeant Terry bellowed. "Grab your gear. Get your rest while you can. At dawn we're going after the escaped prisoner."

The one thing that worried Sergeant Terry, more than the escaped prisoner who he suspected was probably just out hunting for game before the full onset of winter, was the band of Indians they had seen ride out of the camp earlier in the day. Those Indians never returned before dark. They'd ridden east, into the very meadow where the soldiers would be going come morning. Were they scouts? Were they hunters? Sergeant Terry wasn't sure what their purpose was, but he knew if those Indians spotted Lieutenant Fisher's patrol then the whole jig would be up.

- 12 -

Moses Calhoun woke to a pleasant surprise.

Not only had no snow fallen in the night, but the first light of morning shone blue in the night sky, not gray. The clouds had lifted and he could expect to see the sun this day.

With eager anticipation to the warmth of day, Calhoun rose. He returned to his dug-out fire pit and made a small fire for coffee and bacon. He cut away a couple of small pieces of mold from one of the biscuits Kee Kuttai had packed for him and cooked the biscuit in the grease of the bacon. When his food was cooked, he fashioned a spit raised above the fire. While he at his breakfast and drank his coffee, he draped his socks over a stick on the raised spit and left his bare feet near the fire to keep them warm. Moses Calhoun had learned over the years that if he could keep his feet warm and dry, he could suffer any other hardships, and so he always took extra care with his feet and his socks.

By the time the sun broke the horizon, Calhoun was already walking his horse and mule through the timber.

At some point he would be forced to drop down into the meadow because the slope in the timber would prevent him from continuing under the cover of trees, but for now he would remain hidden as long as possible. He knew the soldiers were moving again this morning. They intended their observations to be just one day. As long as he could avoid it, Calhoun did not want to appear down in the valley in the open where he might be seen.

By mid-morning, Calhoun had worked himself onto a deer path that gave him a reasonable opportunity to follow along through the timber on a path that was somewhat cleared, though he still sometimes had to push his way through wet and cold spruce branches.

At some point late in the morning, Calhoun stopped for water. His metal canteen was icy, but the water was not completely frozen. He had the canteen wrapped in a burlap sack that did only a little to insulate it against the cold.

While he drank, Calhoun heard a noise in the trees higher up the slope.

It was a simple rustling noise, not the sort of thing that was unexpected inside a tree line raging with wildlife, and not even as much noise as Calhoun was making with his horse and mule.

His hatchet was hanging loose against his thigh, slid down into a loop tied from his belt. His long rifle was strapped to the pannier on the mule, and the stolen six-shooter from the soldier was stashed inside the pannier.

Calhoun scanned the woods above him, looking for any sign of movement or life that might have explained the noise he heard. It could have simply been collected snow in the top of a spruce melting and breaking loose, falling through the branches. But he did not think so.

He stood quietly beside his horse, one hand rubbing the horse's neck from habit, the other holding the icy canteen. He had taken off his bearskin coat earlier in the morning and draped that over the pannier on the mule's back. Though the day was cold, the exertion of walking in that heavy coat had made him start to sweat, and that made him all the colder.

Seeing nothing, Calhoun slung the canteen back over the saddle horn and took up the lead on the horse and began walking again.

He walked on for some distance until he came to large clearing on the hillside where the spruce forest opened up quite a bit.

At the edge of the clearing, Calhoun spent several minutes watching the valley below for any sign of the soldiers. He knew he was about to be out in the open, and if the soldiers were passing through the meadow below, they would undoubtedly see him. There were a few scattered spruce trees in the clearing, but nothing sufficient to hide him, the horse, and the mule.

As he watched the valley, Calhoun again heard a noise in the forest above him.

That settled his mind.

He was being stalked.

Another mountain lion, perhaps. Maybe a bear looking for one last meal before going in for the winter. The noise seemed too big to be a squirrel or even a large bird, but sometimes it was hard to tell. Sometimes a squirrel could make quite a racket.

With a last look down at the valley below and his hand on the head of his hatchet, Calhoun started out into the clearing, tugging horse and mule behind him.

Whatever was watching him from above the slope would either have to give up the pursuit or expose itself.

Moses Calhoun was twenty yards into the clearing. The snow was melting, and both the horse and mule were dropping their heads to snatch at the tall grass. Just ahead, a large spruce tree blocked much of his view of the valley to the west.

That's where he was when movement in the corner of his eye alerted him to danger.

Calhoun spun around, stepping away from the horse, and jerked the hatchet free.

***

Swift as the wind, the Snake warriors came around him and had Moses Calhoun surrounded.

The seemed to emerge from the air, though Calhoun knew they had come out of the tree line. One of the warriors even managed to get between Calhoun and the lone spruce tree that had been in front of him.

They were Snake warriors, no doubt about that. Calhoun recognized their clothing immediately – pants and shirts of deer hide and long coats made of stitched rabbit fur with elaborate bead work. They carried spears and knives. Two of them had old smoothbore muskets that they aimed at Calhoun.

The mountain hunter raised up his hand, clutching the hatchet high over his head where the Snake warriors could see it clearly.

"Tekaiten Toi-yah'-to'-ko!" he shouted, the same as he did when the mountain lion attacked him.

The Snake men with the muskets lowered them, as did the men with spears and knives. Though all of the men remained on guard. As one, they looked to one of the braves in their number. Calhoun, who had been in this position before, understood why they all looked to the one. He was the one in their group who spoke the best English.

"Cougar Killer," the man said.

Moses Calhoun nodded.

"Tekaiten Toi-yah'-to'-ko," he said again. Speaking the words of their own language to the Snake people, Moses Calhoun was aware of how awkward his voice sounded saying them. But he knew the phrase. It had been repeated to him many times by his wife Kee Kuttai who spoke some of the Snake language, even though she had grown up hearing French from her Canadian father. The Snake people's language was almost as foreign to her as English because her father forbade her mother from speaking it in his presence. "Your chief, Mukuakantun, gave me that name."

The warrior nodded.

"Yes. This story is known to me," he said, his English sounding as unnatural as Moses Calhoun's Snake.

"I am going to your winter camp," Moses said. "I seek Mukuakantun to speak to him."

The warrior squinted, taking his time to make sense of the words that he seldom heard. Then he patted himself on the chest.

"Kee Nangkawitsi Tekaiten," he said.

"That's your name?" Moses asked.

The warrior nodded.

"Kee Nangkawitsi Tekaiten," the Snake warrior repeated. "I can take you to Mukuakantun."

Though he said he would take Moses Calhoun to the chief, the warrior continued to eye him suspiciously, as they all did. The men talked among themselves. Calhoun heard them say his name several times, and he noted their suspicious glances each time his name was uttered. But it was more than suspicion in those glances. There was a bit of curiosity, too, in the looks they gave him.

Calhoun understood their looks. He'd felt them before from Snake men who heard his name. What he did to earn the name was no great feat. Many a man would have done the same. But Mukuakantun was a man who talked freely and loved to tell a story, and every story grew with each new telling – embellishments added for the entertainment of his audience. And over time, the subjects of Mukuakantun's stories became awesome and terrible and larger than life, so that when Snake warriors who heard the story of Tekaiten Toi-yah'-to'-ko, the Lion Killer, they expected if they ever met him to find a man who was seven feet tall and broad as a mountain. The real thing always seemed to surprise, if not disappoint.

The men continued to talk for several minutes, and there seemed to be some disagreement between them.

"We are tekaiten," Kee Nangkawitsi Tekaiten said. "Hunters. We hunt deheyana duku."

He stopped and shrugged, and then put both hands atop his head with his fingers spread very wide, bending slightly so that he resembled an animal with antlers.

"Deer," Moses Calhoun said. "Hunting for deer meat."

The warrior nodded.

"Other men do not want to go back without deer," he said. "Kee Nangkawitsi Tekaiten will take you."

"I can make my own way," Calhoun said.

The Indian shook his head to show he did not understand.

"You stay and hunt," Calhoun said, making hand motions to make himself understood. "I can go alone to the camp."

The warrior shook his head.

"No. Kee Nangkawitsi Tekaiten and Tekaiten Toi-yah'-to'-ko both go."

Calhoun nodded his head, and as he did the other men turned and walked back into the woods. In a moment, one of them brought a horse out from the cover of the trees to Kee Nangkawitsi Tekaiten.

When the other Indians were gone back to their hunting and it was just Moses Calhoun and Kee Nangkawitsi Tekaiten standing in the clearing near the lone spruce, Calhoun said to him, "Have you seen white soldiers?"

Kee Nangkawitsi Tekaiten's eyes grew wide at the

mention of white soldiers. He knew the words plenty well. But he shook his head.

"There are some about," Moses Calhoun said. "A score of them, or so."

The Indian frowned. He was only catching some of what Calhoun said.

"I take you to Mukuakantun," he said.

"We can't ride through the valley," Moses said, pointing down toward the meadow. "We need to stay under the cover of trees." He turned and pointed toward the trees ahead of them.

The Snake warrior shrugged and leapt up onto his horse's back.

Calhoun wasn't sure the man understood him, but he climbed into his own saddle.

Kee Nangkawitsi Tekaiten turned his horse up the slope and rode a little ways through the clearing, and higher up he found a path that was wide enough for both men to ride their horses – evidently he had understood Calhoun's warning and was now leading him along a path that would shield them from view of the soldiers in the valley.

They rode like this for some distance, and then the slope of the mountain became impassible, and the trail dropped back down through the spruce trees to the valley. But even as they rode off the mountain, the spruce forest seemed to spill down from the mountain and go out into the valley some way before it disintegrated into the meadow.

The trail continued through the spruce trees here, hiding their approach to the winter camp almost the entire way.

And then, within a mile of the winter camp, they emerged from the trees into the meadow where the snow was melting, and rode directly to the camp, crossing the river.

- 13 -

"We're fifteen miles or more from the Snakes' winter camp," Lieutenant Fisher said. "No one at the camp will hear our guns."

Sergeant Terry shook his head. He'd voiced his objection, but the lieutenant was determined. Sergeant Terry suspected that Lieutenant Fisher wanted to attack the Snake hunters simply to be able to report back that there was an encounter and the soldiers had been victorious. It would be something, at least, to be able to say that while they lost a prisoner, they engaged with the enemy and came out victorious.

Sergeant Terry's last hope was for Bearclaw Jim to voice an objection, but the man was bloodthirsty.

There were nine of them down there, a small hunting party out making one last search for game before the winter came.

They had stopped to make camp for the night and were huddled under blankets at the base of a cliff.

Lieutenant Fisher, Sergeant Terry, Bearclaw Jim and the Lakota Scout were above them, looking down on them from a ridge. The rest of the soldiers were beyond the ridge, about half a mile back.

The Lakota Scout had been the first to see the hunting party and had come back to make the white soldiers aware.

All day they had tracked their escaped prisoner. He'd made no effort to hide his tracks in the snow through the meadow, and though the snow was already melting by midday, the Lakota, Jack Cut Face, had managed to follow without any trouble.

Then the tracks abandoned the meadow and went up into the spruce forest. It was harder to track the man here, but the Lakota managed to keep them moving.

The escaped prisoner turned west at some point, going back toward the winter camp.

"I knew he would," Bearclaw Jim announced, gleeful in his victory.

And now those tracks had taken the soldiers near to this party of Snake hunters.

Lieutenant Fisher said it was too much to risk letting those men pass in peace. The hunters might easily spot the soldiers, or their tracks, and go back to alert the camp.

"The camp already knows we're here," Bearclaw Jim muttered.

"We don't know that," Lieutenant Fisher said. "But we do know that if these Snake hunters cross our tracks or, worse yet, happen to see us, they will alert the camp."

Sensing it might mean an opportunity for scalping some Injuns, Bearclaw Jim happily agreed that they should wipe them out.

"Sergeant Terry, go back and bring up the men," Lieutenant Fisher whispered. "Bring them on foot, and leave a small guard back with the horses."

Terry nodded and slid back away from the ridge, careful not to make a movement that might catch the attention of the men below.

Dusk was already upon the men, and in the spruce and pine forest, it was even darker.

The Snake hunters had made a fire and were roasting a small animal of some kind, likely a rabbit or two.

After some time, the lieutenant heard the rattle of equipment and the murmur of whispered voices as the men came up. He motioned angrily for them to be silent.

"There are nine men down there," Lieutenant Fisher told his soldiers. "None may be allowed to escape."

Lieutenant Fisher nodded to Sergeant Terry.

The sergeant spread his men out into a ragged battle line. These were poorly trained cavalry men fighting in the frozen woods. They were not infantrymen who were trained and experienced in this sort of fight. Nevertheless, Sergeant Terry trusted that any man smart enough to get into the army was also smart enough to point a revolver in the right direction.

"Cap your pistols," the sergeant said.

The men carried their guns without percussion caps to avoid the chance for an accidental discharge – not that Lieutenant Fisher or anyone else cared if a soldier shot himself. But the officer did not want any of his men to accidentally shoot off a gun and alert nearby hostiles that there were soldiers around.

But now the men took out their revolvers – two a piece – and began rotating the cylinders to push the percussion caps down on the nipples.

Each man had a dozen shots loaded into his guns. There were twenty men, not including those who had stayed back with the horses. Down below there were only nine hostile Indians. Lieutenant Fisher had all the faith in the world that his men would make short work of the Indians.

He drew his cavalry saber from its sheath and raised it up in the air. With a swish, he brought it down, and the men advanced.

They did not rush through the woods. They moved slowly, calmly, going from tree to tree in the hopes of closing the distance on their enemies without being seen.

The soldiers were just twenty yards away from the campfire when one of the Indians saw them.

He reached for a musket and brought it up to his shoulder, and the big gun kicked as it belched out smoke and flame.

The other warriors at the campfire leapt to action, some drawing knives and others grabbing spears or hatchets.

The soldiers charged.

As fast as they could aim and draw back the hammer, the soldiers were firing lead balls into the Indian camp. In moments, three of the Snake hunters were dead.

Now it was a rush through the woods as the Indians fled for their lives. The soldiers chased them, firing as they ran. Bearclaw Jim and the Lakota scout fell upon the dead, their knives slicing their hair from their skulls.

The Indians were smart in that they spread out. Running in different directions gave two, or one, a better chance at escape. The soldiers pooled together in their pursuit. Where one man went, five others followed, chasing down a single Indian until a shot or two or three brought the man to the ground.

When they caught their fallen prey, the soldiers finished them off with a final bullet or a knife blade.

In a minute, the six fleeing Indians were down to just three, and then two.

But the two ran hard.

One jumped from a cliff face. He landed on the rocks twenty feet below and kept running, but the pursuing soldiers wouldn't jump, so they had to find another way down.

The Indian continued to run, fleeing for the open valley below.

He had made distance on his pursuers by jumping the cliff.

The only other Snake Indian from the hunting party still alive had gone up, rather than down. He fled higher up the steep slope, deeper into the spruce forest.

Running through the forest was no strange task for the man. Many times he had mounted these steep slopes in pursuit of elk or deer. The cold air burned his lungs, but his muscles kept his legs pumping.

Three soldiers followed this man.

"Did you see which way he went?" one of them asked, breathing so hard he had to stop. The other two also stopped with him, both breathing just as hard.

"I lost him in the trees."

"I don't see him nowhere."

The first man fired a shot into the ground.

"We'll tell the lieutenant we got him."

Down below, the man making for the meadow broke free of the trees, still running as hard as when he started. He wished he had his horse, but the horse would have never made the jump from the cliff.

He'd gone forty yards, and then fifty, from the tree line. He was more than a hundred yards when at last the first soldier in pursuit broke free from the trees. The man fired a shot, but it was well short.

Now other soldiers came out of the tree line and saw the Snake hunter running through the meadow.

"We'll never catch him," one said. "We need our horses."

"Lieutenant Fisher's going to be fit to be tied when he finds out one of 'em got away."

The soldiers returned to the others. They'd not suffered any casualties in the assault, but Lieutenant Fisher was raging about the man who escaped into the valley. Quickly, he had several of his men mount up on their horses and start moving toward the valley.

"We'll ride him down," Fisher said.

In the valley, the soldiers spread out and rode hard. There was almost no daylight left, but they soon caught sight of the man in the distance.

Lieutenant Fisher drew his saber and brought his horse to a gallop. Raising up in the stirrups, the lieutenant rode down the fleeing Snake hunter, thrashing him with his sword.

The man, exhausted and full of fright, fell to the ground.

Lieutenant Fisher wheeled his horse and rode back. He dismounted and ran the Indian through with his saber.

With a satisfied grin, he looked up at his men who were catching up to him now.

"We can report a successful encounter with the enemy," he said. "If we can track down our escaped prisoner, we can return to the regiment with our information and this entire expedition will be a success."

***

Fisher and those soldiers who had followed him rode back toward the forest, back to where Sergeant Terry and the rest of the men waited.

When they returned, they found Bearclaw Jim in a heated conversation with the Lakota scout, and Sergeant Terry standing nearby. Fisher rode directly over to where the men were standing.

"We finished off the last of them," Lieutenant Fisher said from the saddle.

"Maybe not," Sergeant Terry said.

"How's that?" Fisher demanded.

"The scout here, Jack Cut Face, he says he's tracked one and believes he got away."

Fisher's heart sank. Given a small task – to reconnoiter the winter camp – and a sole command, Fisher had managed to make a mess of it. He felt that he'd not done anything wrong. His men had failed him at every turn. They failed to keep the prisoner. They failed to kill all of the Indians in the hunting party. He himself had been forced to ride down and kill one escapee, and now he learned there was a second man to escape.

"He's surely gone back to the winter camp," Bearclaw Jim said.

Lieutenant Fisher swung himself down from his saddle and stamped his foot on the ground.

"How, by God, did one of them escape?"

Sergeant Terry muttered something about "confusion of battle." None of the men who had chased the Indian were willing to fess up to their part in his escape, and Sergeant Terry was willing to believe the man had slipped off without pursuit.

Darkness had settled around them by now. They couldn't give chase now, and under the cover of darkness the man would be able to make the winter camp.

- 14 -

The arrival of a white man in the winter camp created a moment of excitement, especially for the children but for everyone else, as well.

They'd seen him coming and recognized Moses Calhoun as a white man even from a distance. The saddled horse and the mule with a pannier were the easy giveaways, but even atop his horse he didn't sit like an Indian. By the time they reached the eastern bank of the river, already there were many children and even several armed men gathered on the western bank.

The meadow grass seemed to roll right into the river, and it was just a slight step for the horses from bank to river bottom. The mule stopped and would not budge, even with Calhoun pulling on the lead rope.

"Come on you danged varmint," Moses Calhoun shouted at it, and the children on the opposite bank laughed uproariously.

Moses Calhoun was not a vain man. In the harsh mountains where every decision had to be made with a thought to survival, there was no time for a man to think overmuch about a thing such as pride. Nevertheless, any hope Tekaiten Toi-yah'-to'-ko might have had of making a grand river crossing and impressing the Snake People was gone with a buck and a bellow from the stubborn mule.

At last, with an aggravated heave on the lead rope, Calhoun convinced the mule to come along.

Kee Nangkawitsi Tekaiten had gone ahead across the river and settled the men who were ready to meet the white stranger with weapons, and so as Moses's horse stepped up the west bank, he was greeted largely by laughing children – laughing because the mule again refused to step out of the river.

Calhoun had to grin at himself as he looked around at the laughing children.

"You didn't want to get your damned feet wet, and now you don't want to get them dry," he scolded the mule. The children laughed appreciatively.

At last, one of the men who had stayed around to watch walked over to the bank and held his hands out for the lead rope. Calhoun handed it to him, and the man gave a tug and the mule came right up the bank. With a self-satisfied grin, the Indian handed the lead rope back to Calhoun.

"Come," Kee Nangkawitsi Tekaiten called to him, and Calhoun followed the man back toward the teepees that were set up near the spruce trees west of the camp.

He picketed the horse and mule on long leads that would give them plenty of space to graze and he removed the saddle and blanket from the horse and then unpacked the mule. Kee Nangkawitsi Tekaiten did not offer to help, but stood and watched him the entire time.

The sun had disappeared behind the western mountains, though there was still light in the sky and daylight left in the day when Calhoun finished with his animals.

Kee Nangkawitsi Tekaiten started to lead him back to a large teepee, but they did not get far before an elderly man stepped out, a broad smile on his face, and walked toward Moses Calhoun with his arms extended.

The old man pulled him into an embrace and then stepped back to look at him. Chief Mukuakantun remained strong and lithe on his feet, but he had aged much since Calhoun had last seen him. His once-black hair had turned mostly gray, and deep wrinkles lined his face. He had added some weight around his middle.

"My white brother," Chief Mukuakantun said. "Tekaiten Toi-yah'-to'-ko, you are welcome to our camp."

"It is good to see you, Mukuakantun," Calhoun said.

"Come into the warmth and let us talk," Mukuakantun said.

The teepee was very large on the inside, with bearskins laid out as rugs to keep the cold from coming up through the ground. A small fire burned at the center of the teepee, and though it was small, the fire gave a tremendous warmth so that Calhoun had to slide out of his buckskin shirt. The teepee could easily have held a dozen men, but Chief Mukuakantun and Moses Calhoun were now the only two in it.

Calhoun had been around the Snake people enough that he knew their customs. There was a formal dance that had to be made, especially with Chief Mukuakantun, before he could get to the reason for his visit.

So the two men spoke at length about the scarcity of game in recent years. Mukuakantun offered predictions for the coming winter, which he said would be cold and long. It was the same prediction the man made of every winter, but it would be hard for anyone to prove he'd ever been wrong.

"Settlers have had livestock stolen from them," Calhoun said when Mukuakantun had made his predictions of deep snows lasting for many weeks.

"Yes," the old chief agreed.

"Travelers on the white man's trails have been killed," Calhoun said.

"I have heard such stories," Mukuakantun said.

"The white soldiers are very angry and will come to make war," Moses Calhoun said.

It was as much as he would say. Mukuakantun was a friend, but Calhoun had decided that it was not his place to warn the Snake People. If a band of Snake warriors decided to come to his cabin and steal his livestock or take his wife and scalp his children, Mukuakantun would not warn him. It was their way not to interfere, even for a friend.

"They will come to make war," the chief agreed. "We have prepared for such a thing. But we will be gone when snows melt, and we will scatter like dust against wind."

Calhoun nodded.

"The white men are fighting each other in the East," Calhoun said. "They sometimes fight even in the winter."

Mukuakantun shook his head.

"They will not come to make war in winter," he said.

Calhoun nodded, understanding why Mukuakantun would believe such a thing. For many years, the winter camp was a place of safety for the Snake People and other tribes because the white soldiers did not venture out for battle from their own winter quarters.

"They might," Moses said.

"Have you come so far to speak to me about white soldiers?" Mukuakantun asked.

Moses shook his head.

"No. I have not come to talk of white soldiers. You have a woman in your camp who is the daughter of a friend," Moses Calhoun said. "Her name is Aka Ne'ai. I have come to speak to her."

Mukuakantun narrowed his eyes and studied Calhoun for some time.

"Eli Simmons is her father," Mukuakantun said.

"Yes. A friend to me ever since I came into these mountains. He's living in a white town, now, and he asked me to bring his daughter to him with her children."

Mukuakantun nodded his head thoughtfully for a moment, still watching Moses Calhoun closely.

"She is wife of Kee Nangkawitsi Tekaiten," he said.

Moses cocked his head. "The man who brought me into the camp?"

"He is the one."

"That's why his English is good," Moses said.

"She speaks the white man's tongue to him," Mukuakantun said. "She speaks to me, also, and helps me to make the words."

"Your English is very good, Chief Mukuakantun," Moses Calhoun said.

Several men now came to the teepee, and Mukuakantun invited them in. They sat in a circle around the fire, all facing each other. It was eight men, plus their chief and Moses Calhoun, and the teepee became almost uncomfortably warm. They men brought food with them that they passed around, meat and flat breads. Moses was grateful for something to eat, but careful not to take too much. He had his own provisions, and none of the people in the winter village appeared to be well fed.

Moses noted that one of the men who had come in with them was Kee Nangkawitsi Tekaiten, the husband of Eli Simmons's daughter. But Chief Mukuakantun made no more mention of Aka Ne'ai or of Calhoun's desire to talk to her.

Instead, he began to tell the men the story of how their chief and Moses Calhoun first became friends.

He would tell them a piece of the story, and then look to Moses and repeat in English what he had told the others.

"I tell them that we met many winters ago in the forest," he said. "I tell them that you were hunting, and I

133

had my son with me to teach him to hunt."

Calhoun nodded at the memory.

Chief Mukuakantun began to speak to his people again, using big gestures with his arms to elaborate his story. At parts, the men laughed. At other parts, they looked in wonder at Moses Calhoun.

"I tell them that my son had wandered away from me, down near a river, while I watched a draw waiting for deer to move within reach of my bow. And that was when the cougars attacked my son. A pack of them set upon him. But you were there, watching the same draw but down at the bottom. And you rushed forward, leaping like the cougars, catching them as they tried to pounce upon my son. Slashing at them with your knife."

Moses Calhoun laughed.

"Chief, the years have confused you," Calhoun said with a grin. "It was just the one mountain lion."

The old chief grinned and shrugged.

"Maybe it was fewer than I remember. But you wrestled them, however many it was. And did the cougar not slash you across your chest with its claws?"

Calhoun nodded.

"It did," he said.

"Show my men so they might believe," he said.

Moses shook his head.

"That hardly seems like it would be necessary, Chief Mukuakantun."

"Go on," the chief persisted. "Show them your scars."

Reluctantly, Moses Calhoun lifted his shirt and bared

his chest.

Even now, so many years later, the scars were evident. Slash marks going one way and then another.

The chief pointed to Calhoun's chest and said something to his warriors, and several of them leaned forward to get a better look at Calhoun's chest.

"I tell them the evidence is there. One clawed you from left, and one clawed you from right."

Moses let down his shirt.

"I recall it being a slash with a left claw and then a slash with the right claw, each claw belonging to the same cat," Moses said.

"If not six, maybe it was three," Chief Mukuakantun laughed.

He spoke again, swinging and jabbing with an imaginary knife.

"I tell them how you wrestled with the cougars and stabbed them and cut them and how you fought the cougars as if you were a cougar yourself."

That part of it, at least, rang true in Calhoun's memory. It had been a chaotic fight. The mountain lion was vicious in its attack, and Calhoun had wrestled it, slashed at it with his Bowie knife, and stabbed it many times before at last it fell dead.

But Calhoun had been badly injured. Chief Mukuakantun put him on a horse and brought him back to camp, and there Calhoun had stayed for two weeks. Chief Mukuakantun's wife had dressed his wounds and changed his bandages. She nursed him through a fever. It was then that he became known among the Snake People as Tekaiten Toi-yah'-to'-ko, the Killer of Mountain Lions.

Chief Mukuakantun also gave Moses the hatchet he now carried, decorated with leather and beadwork that any Snake would immediately recognize.

Over the years, the chief and the white hunter crossed paths several times. Each time, their friendship was renewed. The chief often told the story to his people of how Moses Calhoun, Tekaiten Toi-yah'-to'-ko, had saved his son, and the story had become something of a legend among the People.

Presenting the hatchet to Snake warriors had a couple of times saved Moses's life.

Reliving the story, or Chief Mukuakantun's version of it, and being filled with those emotions of friendship, Moses Calhoun became convinced to change his mind. He decided in that moment that he must warn his old friend that the white soldiers were coming.

"I have something to say to you," Calhoun interrupted, and all of the men turned their attention to him, even those who could not understand what he said. "My reason for coming to your camp is to speak to the woman Aka Ne'ai who is the daughter of my friend. I want to say to her that the white soldiers are coming to make war on the winter camp. Her father, my friend Eli Simmons, wants her with her family to leave the camp and come with me to safety."

Calhoun, who knew that the woman's husband was in the audience, looked deliberately at Kee Nangkawitsi Tekaiten.

"But I want to say to you, Chief Mukuakantun, who is also my friend, that the white soldiers are coming. They are coming now and will be here within the week. They bring many soldiers with good guns, and they seek to punish the Snake People for the thefts and killings of the

white settlers. They have warrants to arrest
Mukuakantun and others, but they will make no attempt
to arrest anyone. They will simply charge the camp and
kill all they can."

Chief Mukuakantun drew a heavy breath and
watched the thin veil of gray smoke rise up out of his
teepee.

"A week?" he said.

"Give or take," Moses Calhoun said. "Maybe ten
days."

Chief Mukuakantun looked to Kee Nangkawitsi
Tekaiten and spoke words that Calhoun did not
understand, and the man spoke back to him.

"Silent Hunter says you may speak to his wife. If she
wishes to go with her children, you may take her."

"All of your people should leave this place," Moses
Calhoun said, frustrated that Mukuakantun did not seem
to understand the severity of what he was being told.

The old man nodded, thoughtfully. The gaiety had
left his face. The lines seemed more thoroughly etched.
The glint in his eyes when he told the story of the rescue
of his son had now dimmed.

"You should make your preparations to leave the
camp," Moses Calhoun said. "Move higher into the
mountains."

Mukuakantun spoke to Kee Nangkawitsi Tekaiten at
some length, and the younger man stood up, looking
expectantly at Calhoun.

"My friend," Mukuakantun said. "Go now with Silent
Hunter, the man we call Kee Nangkawitsi Tekaiten. He
will take you to your things and you can put them in a

teepee where you may spend the night. He will come to you with his wife and their children so that you may speak to her. I, and the other elders of my tribe, will speak tonight of this news you have brought to us."

***

Moses Calhoun explained to Aka Ne'ai the reason for his visit to the Snake winter camp.

They sat in a much smaller teepee. It was cold in there. Though Kee Nangkawitsi Tekaiten built a small fire in the center and there were bearskin rugs for them to sit on, the teepee was already cold when they first came in, and it was not so packed with people that it quickly warmed. While he waited for the fire to grow and begin to warm the teepee, Moses Calhoun sat with his bearskin coat draped over his shoulders.

He told her about Eli Simmons coming to him. He told her about the soldiers who took him prisoner. He told her that her father wanted her to come to him in the town.

Kee Nangkawitsi Tekaiten – Silent Hunter in English – listened to all that Moses said to his wife, sometimes asking her to explain a word or a phrase or a thought that he did not understand.

When Moses was finished with his story, the man and woman spoke at length in their native tongue. Their conversation turned heated a couple of times, but Aka Ne'ai did not persist in arguing with her husband. Then, after some time, she turned back to the man they knew as Cougar Killer, Tekaiten Toi-yah'-to'-ko.

"Silent Hunter says I must go with you," Aka Ne'ai said. "He wants me to take the children and go to my father, and he said he will come for me in the spring."

Moses nodded. He knew that the woman had protested against it, and he knew that the decision to leave her husband to an unknown fate caused her deep pain.

"In the spring, if Silent Hunter comes to Cougar Killer, will Cougar Killer take him to the town where my father lives?"

Calhoun nodded.

"Of course I will," he said.

"They will not leave the camp," Aka Ne'ai said. She spoke quickly, and softly, so that her husband would not catch her words, and Moses knew that this was a conversation between her and him, her husband did not know what she was saying. "They will trust the snow to pile so high that the soldiers cannot come. But the snow in the meadow, it melts now."

Tears rolled silently down the woman's cheeks.

"Anything can happen," Moses said, not knowing what else to say. "Maybe they will move the camp higher into the mountains."

She shook her head.

"They will not move. I know their moods. The young men, like my husband, they want to fight. The old men, they are tired from running."

Moses nodded. He understood the perspective of both, and he could not blame either. But he knew, too, that the Snake People would be destroyed if they stayed to face the soldiers.

"Maybe the snow will come," he said.

- 15 -

Just before dawn an exhausted Snake hunter crossed the river and came into the winter camp. Once he was clear of the soldiers, he alternated between walking and running, following the high trail through the forest until he was forced into the meadow. There, he began to run again.

By the time he collapsed into his brother's teepee, he was spent, too fatigued to do any more than say to his brother that there were soldiers coming.

In a matter of moments, several of the chiefs were

gathering in the brother's teepee, and other men of the tribe came, too, to stand outside and hear what was being said. The word passed quickly from the teepee to the crowd, and the story spread of soldiers in the woods attacking the hunting party. The man said it was a slaughter. All the others had been killed, or so he believed.

And then he made a damning accusation.

Tekaiten Toi-yah'-to-ko had led the soldiers to the valley of the winter camp, he said.

Chief Mukuakantun demanded proof to support the accusation, but quickly others began to support the theory.

Moses Calhoun, the one they called Cougar Killer, was taken by the hunters not far from where the soldiers attacked the hunting party. It seemed all too obvious, to some, that Calhoun was a scout for the soldiers, and when he was captured, he conjured the story about coming for the white trapper's daughter.

Chief Mukuakantun and others spoke against the accusation.

Kee Nangkawitsi Tekaiten stood outside the teepee listening, and quickly saw how the other men became persuaded by the notion that Moses Calhoun was working for the soldiers.

He stepped away from the crowd of men and then hurried to the teepee where his wife and children slept. He woke Aka Ne'ai and told her to move quickly, to get herself and the children ready.

Whatever debate was taking place among the chiefs and the other men, Kee Nangkawitsi Tekaiten believed Moses Calhoun. He believed the soldiers were coming, and he wanted his wife and children taken to safety. He would stay and do his part for the tribe, and if he survived, he would go and find Aka Ne'ai in the white man's town. If he did not survive, he would die knowing that his children lived on.

While his wife woke the children and prepared them to travel, Kee Nangkawitsi Tekaiten went quickly to get three ponies from among the livestock. He tied the ponies with war bridles, a simple cord looped around the horses' lower jaws. The women and children would throw blankets over the backs of the ponies.

By the time he arrived back at his teepee with the horses, Aka Ne'ai and the children were waiting outside. Kee Nangkawitsi Tekaiten left her with the ponies and went to Moses Calhoun's teepee.

The white hunter was already awake, having heard the disturbance as the chiefs gathered earlier.

"You leave now," Kee Nangkawitsi Tekaiten said.

Calhoun, who had guessed some trouble was coming, nodded his head. He gathered up his gear and Kee Nangkawitsi Tekaiten helped him to get his pack to the horse and mule. Kee Nangkawitsi Tekaiten, who did not use a saddle or a pack mule, stood by and watched while Calhoun prepared his animals.

Aka Ne'ai and the children soon walked their ponies over to her husband.

The family exchanged sad goodbyes while Calhoun packed the mule and then saddled his horse.

At last he was ready to go, and he walked his horse and mule over to Eli Simmons's daughter and her husband.

"Kee Nangkawitsi Tekaiten says the soldiers attacked the others of the hunting party," Aka Ne'ai told Calhoun. "Some of the men believe you led the soldiers to our camp."

Calhoun looked at Kee Nangkawitsi Tekaiten.

"It's not true," he said. "The soldiers took me prisoner, as I told you."

Kee Nangkawitsi Tekaiten nodded.

"Go," he said. "Go with Aka Ne'ai and my children."

Calhoun stepped into his saddle. Kee Nangkawitsi Tekaiten helped his wife and children to the backs of their ponies.

There was moonlight enough to see the way, and in places the snow had not completely melted, and the snow glowed white against the dark ground.

They crossed the river, moving slowly so that the horses could step easy and find their footing. Across the river, Calhoun increased the pace.

If the soldiers attacked the hunting party, that meant the soldiers were still somewhere in the valley. And Calhoun knew, too, that if they were in the valley it was because they were looking for him and had likely tracked him back toward the winter camp.

"You keep an eye on your children and do not let them wander or get left behind," Calhoun called back to Aka Ne'ai. "You let them ride between us. Keep them close to me. When dawn comes, we will ride fast to get out of this valley."

At the camp, the chiefs decided to confront Moses Calhoun and allow him to defend himself against the accusation. And so they sent a group of men to the teepee where he was supposed to be sleeping, but when the men returned without him, some among them took that as proof of his guilt.

The discussion continued with Kee Nangkawitsi Tekaiten standing outside again, listening to what was being reported by those who could hear.

He knew that the tribe's chiefs would not come to a quick decision about anything. Every man within the teepee would be given an opportunity to speak his mind, and each point would be talked over incessantly. The way the chiefs reached a decision always inflamed the younger men who were eager for a conclusion, but ever since the tribe had been forced to forage in smaller, separate bands, they had suffered from too many heads.

Though Kee Nangkawitsi Tekaiten had many times been among those frustrated by the slowness of the decision making within the tribe, today he was grateful for it. Every moment that the chiefs argued or overstated a position granted his wife and children time to extend their run to safety.

Safety from the white man within the bosom of the white man.

Kee Nangkawitsi Tekaiten wondered if he had made a mistake in sending his family away.

Above them a light began to appear in the eastern sky. Faint and gray at first, but growing. Soon the teepees became visible in the morning light. And then the ponies and stolen livestock in the meadow beyond the camp. And then the mountains around them took form.

With the first light of dawn now giving shape to the land, the chiefs at last reached a decision.

A patrol would be sent to determine the strength of

the soldiers who attacked the hunting party. If possible, the soldiers would be killed or captured. The patrol would also look for Moses Calhoun to bring him back to the winter camp to answer for the charges against him.

Many among the men believed that when they found the patrol, they would also find the man they called Tekaiten Toi-yah'-to'-ko.

The chiefs broke up and went their separate ways.

Kee Nangkawitsi Tekaiten waited until he saw Chief Mukuakantun walk off alone toward the river bank.

The old chief watched the empty meadow for a long time.

Dawn came with gray clouds overhead, and a bitter cold fog hanging over the valley.

The old chief wrapped his blanket around himself tighter. He sensed the presence of the young warrior coming to him and did not need to turn to know who it was.

In their language, the chief and the young man spoke.

"During the counsel I woke Tekaiten Toi-yah'-to'-ko," Kee Nangkawitsi Tekaiten said. "I sent him away with my wife and children."

The old chief nodded.

"I suspected as much. It was right what you did, my son. Tekaiten Toi-yah'-to'-ko would not deceive his friends. He saved your life many years ago, and he now saves the lives of your children and my grandchildren. I fear with the soldiers coming, your children may be the last of our tribe."

Kee Nangkawitsi Tekaiten squinted into the valley. A

thin veil of fog spread out across it, though he could still see some distance into the valley. There was no sign of the mountain hunter.

"May he ride swift and take my family to safety," Kee Nangkawitsi Tekaiten said.

Even as they stood watching the empty valley with its slight haze of fog, two dozen warriors splashed out into the shallow river. A couple of them let loose with a war whoop. The men were armed with muskets and other weapons, ready to confront soldiers or the mountain hunter, whoever they came to first.

- 16 -

In the darkness it had been difficult for Moses Calhoun to find the high mountain trail that cut through the spruce and pine forest, the one that Kee Nangkawitsi Tekaiten had used to bring Calhoun to the winter camp. But with the soldiers wandering somewhere in the valley, Moses did not want to get caught in the wide, open meadow that stretched for many miles to the mountain pass. And so he scouted along the northern tree line, seeking for the trail until he found it.

It was his horse, really, that found the trail. As they were riding along, Moses keeping the horse to a slow walk, the sorrel dragged his head to the left and started to turn. At first, Moses pulled the horse away, but he was insistent. And that's when Calhoun recognized the trail entrance, the hook of the tree line illuminated in the moonlight. He remembered coming off the trail here. Horses, when given the opportunity, would find their way home.

If riding through the meadow in the darkness had been a slow and difficult task, it proved almost impossible to ride in darkness along the high trail, narrow and with trees on either side and roots and holes to trip the horses underfoot. The small group made poor time as the horses mounted the trail, ascending the long path, following its switchbacks, and finally reaching the high ridge.

They rode some distance in the last of the predawn morning. Calhoun could feel the wet air against his exposed skin, and he knew that a fog had descended down over the valley. It would be a cold morning, and a cold day, and he had a suspicion that yesterday gave them the last they would see of the sun for some time.

"What are the children's names?" Moses asked.

Aka Ne'ai told him that the children had not yet been named. That was common enough among the Snake People. They frequently waited until children were almost into their teens before naming them.

The two boys were slightly older than Moses's own. They looked to be around eight-years-old and maybe six-years-old. They rode their ponies well enough, though the ponies were both old and didn't have much interest in taking off at a gallop.

"How long has it been since you've seen your father?" Moses asked.

"He came into our camp two springs ago," Aka Ne'ai said. "He'd come looking for me because he'd taken sick over that winter and was not sure he would see me again. So he came looking because he wanted to see his grandchildren."

"He cares for you very much," Moses said. "When he came to ask me to come and find you, I could see that he was worried."

Aka Ne'ai smiled sadly.

"He is a good man, but not a very good father," she said. "When my mother died, he did not know what to do with me. So he took me to her people."

"You've done well with them," Calhoun said. "You have a good husband, good children."

"Married to a chief's son," she said.

Calhoun twisted in his saddle and glanced over his shoulder at her.

"A chief's son?" he asked.

"Silent Hunter is the son of Chief Mukuakantun," she said.

"So he is the boy I saved all those years ago?" Moses asked, incredulous.

"Silent Hunter, my husband Kee Nangkawitsi Tekaiten, is the boy you saved."

It seemed impossible that the young boy had grown old so fast, and even now had children older than Moses's own children. But Moses Calhoun knew, too, he had grown older in that time. What had it been? Fifteen years maybe. The boy he saved would have been about fifteen at the time, making Kee Nangkawitsi Tekaiten thirty-years-old now. And fifteen years ago, Moses Calhoun was close to that same age. He was twenty-seven or twenty-eight when he saved the Indian boy from the mountain lion.

"So many years, gone by so fast," Calhoun said, wondering at the way the winter days seemed to move so slowly at the time, but now seemed to have evaporated in an instant.

Intermittently, the trail opened up into small clearings, or it widened into narrow meadows.

In these spaces, Calhoun could judge the increasing snowfall. Big, wet flakes were falling now. Under the canopy of the trees along the trail, the snow still wasn't making it down to the ground, but in the open spaces it was falling at a tremendous rate.

"We won't make the pass today," Calhoun told Aka Ne'ai. "But we need to get through it tomorrow as early as we can. The snow will pile faster and deeper in the pass, and we'll find it difficult going if we linger much beyond tomorrow morning."

The woman did not bother to respond. She had the looped bridle cord in one hand, and she pinched a blanket that she had wrapped around her with the other hand. She now squeezed it tighter.

The boys were loving their big adventure and oblivious to the cold, but Aka Ne'ai kept reminding them to cover their heads.

Around midday, Moses Calhoun's sorrel stepped out into a wide patch of the trail where the ridge ran straight and level for sixty yards. A couple of squat fir trees interrupted the view from one end of the clearing to the other, but for the most part it was a straight shot through the clearing from one end of the meadow to the other.

The view was gray with fog and falling snow, and Calhoun realized that the snow was coming faster and harder now, and the flakes smaller. Big flakes, like big rain drops, often meant it would not last. But these smaller flakes suggested the snow would continue to pile for hours. Perhaps even off and on through the next few days.

At first, in the snow and fog, Calhoun did not understand exactly what he was seeing. Just shadows in the fog and heavy snowfall. He thought that farther along the trail he could see a small herd of buffalo. He'd seen buffalo in the woods before, but it was an uncommon sight, and especially so far up the slope like this.

But when the surprise of seeing something on the trail ahead of them subsided, Calhoun realized he was seeing horsemen.

"Damnation," he muttered to himself.

He did not think that the men ahead had seen them, but they would momentarily.

He swung quickly from his saddle and took four steps back to the pack mule where he pulled his sheathed rifle from the pack. The boys had pulled their horses to a halt, and Aka Ne'ai's eyes had grown wide with worry.

"Soldiers ahead," Calhoun said.

He looked at the slope below the ridge that dropped through the trees down toward the meadow. They could walk their horses, but would never be able to ride their horses at that steep slope with so many branches in the way. There was no clear trail – not even a deer path.

Calhoun profoundly felt the burden of his responsibility. A woman and two children – not his own – that he had promised to protect.

"There was a drawback half a mile or so," Calhoun said to Aka Ne'ai. "You understand? A draw – an easy slope down to the valley. Take the children and ride back to the place. Go quickly, and do not look back. When you get to the valley, go east, toward the pass. Hurry, now."

The woman nodded and called to her children to follow her.

Calhoun looked back, watching for the soldiers. The fir trees growing in the middle of the valley interrupted their view of him, but there were so many soldiers riding in single file, that they made an easier sight than Calhoun, his horse and mule.

Loading a flintlock rifle was no quick process, but Calhoun had practice. Elk and deer seldom stood around waiting for a hunter to take his time loading his rifle, and as a man who survived on what he could shoot, Moses Calhoun had learned to load and prime his rifle with speed.

So he quickly loaded the long Tennessee rifle, pouring powder and ramming the ball home. He poured out a bit of powder into the pan and cocked back the flintlock hammer.

Moses Calhoun had no fight with the soldiers, but he expected they thought they had a fight with him.

He turned the horse, moving as fast as he could with his rifle gripped in one hand. The mule followed, his lead tied to the horse's saddle horn. Walking backwards so that he could keep an eye on the distant grayness, waiting for the shadows to reappear.

With the horse turned back down the trail, Calhoun gave its hindquarter a slap. Nothing hard enough to spook it or make it bolt, but enough that hopefully the horse would move. And with a glance over its shoulder at him, the sorrel started to walk, following in the path behind the Aka Ne'ai and the two boys.

At least that would put the horse and mule out of the line of fire if this were to turn into a shooting war.

Calhoun took several steps forward, crouched low. He stepped off the trail, huddling behind the trunk of a lodgepole pine.

He dropped down to one knee and raised up the barrel of the Tennessee rifle. "Poor-boy," they called it. Poor it may be, but that rifle had fed him – and now his family – for many years. The rifle had protected him, bringing down buffalo and elk, bear and deer. He'd shot a fair number of Indians with the rifle, and a couple of white men, too.

Behind the rifle that others called "Poor-boy," Moses Calhoun had survived.

He intended to keep on surviving.

***

Several moments passed, and still the soldiers did not appear at the far end of the trail.

Moses Calhoun squinted into the snow and fog. Surely by now he should be able to see them. Even low, below the branches of the fir trees in the path, he did not see the horses' hooves.

He drew a slow, even breath, the stock of the heavy gun in his shoulder, the weight of it supported in his left hand, his finger lightly touching the trigger. He was ready to shoot if the soldiers forced him to. He had the six-shooter tucked in his belt, and his knife and hatchet also. His plan was to buy Aka Ne'ai time to get a ways down that draw. A minute, two minutes if he could. And then, if necessary, he would fight a running battle through the woods.

He swung around to a noise in the trees off the path, the barrel of the gun seeking out the threat, a target. Ten yards above him, among the trees, he saw Bearclaw Jim grinning at him. The scout was flanked by soldiers on each side.

"Hold your fire boys!" Bearclaw Jim shouted, grinning like the devil, what teeth he had in his head stained and jagged. "Lieutenant! We got your prisoner back!"

Bearclaw Jim stood up from a crouched position, and took a step into the open. He held in his fist a large Bowie knife.

"Go on and throw down that gun, boy. We've got you surrounded."

"No, sir," Moses Calhoun shouted back. He heard a noise below him. Some of the soldiers were moving off the trail down below, coming up from behind him.

"No, sir," Calhoun repeated. "I'll not be taken prisoner today. Now, I've got no fight with you or them soldiers, but if you press me, I'll press back. You understand?"

"Throw down that rifle, Calhoun," Lieutenant Fisher called.

He was down below Calhoun, maybe twenty or twenty-five yards away. Unlike Bearclaw Jim, the lieutenant did not expose himself. Calhoun glanced back and could see the officer's saber, drawn and sticking out from behind a pine where the lieutenant had sought shelter. Calhoun could see at least a couple of men down with the lieutenant.

As he glanced back to Bearclaw Jim, he saw other soldiers making their way slowly, cautiously, along the trail.

They were above and below him, and in front of him on the trail. But they were not yet behind him, and Calhoun intended to keep it that way.

"You men move back and allow me to pass, and you'll live to see nightfall," Calhoun shouted, saying the words loud enough so that all the men could hear.

Bearclaw Jim spoke softly to a couple of the men, and they started to work their way down the path to get in behind Calhoun. Those men would cut off any opportunity he had for escape.

Calhoun pulled the trigger. The flint fell. The powder in the pan flared.

The .50 caliber bullet broke the Bowie knife in half and flew from the scout's hand. The lead ball took with the knife Bearclaw Jim's forefinger and thumb, and a healthy chunk from his palm.

The man hollered like a wounded cougar, clutching with his good hand at the stumps left behind by Calhoun's shot.

None among the soldiers expected the mountain hunter to shoot. He was facing two dozen men. So for just a moment, every man in the woods except one was caught off guard by the sudden, reckless shot.

In that moment, Moses Calhoun turned and leapt from the ridge into the branches of a spruce tree. He clutched his rifle close to him and rolled through the branches.

The slope here was too steep for the horses, but it was perfect for a headlong run toward the valley.

Calhoun rolled through the branches and landed on the ground, already sliding along the wet pine straw blanket on the ground. He kept his feet and slid in a crouch. His shoulder hit hard against a pine trunk, and above him there was an explosion of gunfire.

Calhoun slid quickly around the trunk, putting the tree between him and the soldiers. Then he leapt and ran a short ways to the next tree. He slung himself around to the downslope side of the tree trunk and shifted his rifle from his left hand to his right.

The shooting behind him subsided some. The soldiers were beginning to pursue him down the slope. A couple of soldiers tried a shot at him. One skinned the bark on the tree.

Calhoun turned to his left and ran another ten yards. He jumped a fallen tree and landed on wet pine straw. His feet slid out from under him and he crashed hard against the ground.

He used his rifle to push himself off the ground and took a glance behind him.

He pulled the Colt Navy from his belt and took aim at one of the soldiers even as he cocked the hammer on the gun. He let fly a second shot. This one struck a soldier in the thigh. The man yelped and tumbled over.

Moses Calhoun winced. That wound would probably prove fatal in these mountains. Maybe down near a town or an army doctor something could be done for him, if nothing else a doctor could cut the leg off. But in these mountains the man would either bleed to death or an infection would take hold.

Calhoun did not wait to see if the man would try to regain his feet or if his comrades would come to his aid.

The mountain hunter ran again, covering his face with his forearms and using the long rifle to bat away spruce branches that lashed at his face as he ran.

Again, he heard a few shots behind him, but he did not stop to see where they were hitting.

He jumped a small drop and found himself in a clearing. The forest here was thinning, and down below him, through the fog and snow, Calhoun could see the draw. Aka Ne'ai was there, with the two boys. The sorrel and mule were following behind her. She'd heard the shooting and was hurrying the horses at a trot.

It was still some distance from where she was in the draw to the valley meadow. The soldiers had come at him unhorsed. If Moses could get the woman and children to the meadow, they might be able to ride hard and gain some distance.

Even as he had the thought, he knew he would have to abandon the mule and the supplies they would need to get back to his home.

Hoping to gain another moment, or two, Calhoun turned with the revolver and sought a target.

As he did, there was an almighty volley – it sounded like a hundred rifles, not just two dozen. The mountain hunter waited, expecting to feel a dozen shots punch through his body.

But the shots never came.

There was more shooting up above. Intense shooting

that sounded like a battle, not a pursuit.

Calhoun did not wait to understand.

He charged forward, breaking into the clearing, running down the slope and down into the draw.

Aka Ne'ai saw him running and let out and yelp.

"Ride!" Calhoun yelled at her.

He made a leap down into the narrow bottom of the draw and grabbed hold of the sorrel's reins.

He unwrapped the mule's lead and pulled the mule up to him. He snatched his heavy bearskin coat from the top of the pannier, and his possibles bag.

He stepped into the stirrup and used his reins to get the sorrel moving so that he could catch Eli Simmons's daughter and grandchildren.

- 17 -

Chris Dolan was standing beside Bearclaw Jim when Moses Calhoun fired the shot that took the man's finger and thumb.

Private Dolan, like his brother and the other troopers, gaped in shock – shock at the severed fingers and the howl of the wounded man; shock that Calhoun would try a shot with so many guns pointing at him; shock that he moved so quickly and seemed to vanish into the spruce boughs.

And then someone shouted an order to fire, and two

dozen guns erupted, sending a curtain of lead down into the forest after the man.

Some of the soldiers started to pursue Calhoun.

Dolan, being closest to Bearclaw Jim, bent to help the man who had sunk to his knees, but with a hand covered in his own blood, Bearclaw Jim pushed Dolan away.

"Leave me be!" he snarled.

Dolan backed away, not sure what to do.

Some of the men were making a dash through the woods after their former prisoner. Others were looking back to their horses, uncertain if they should mount or go on foot.

Dolan wasn't sure if it was moments or minutes. Time seemed to stop having any meaning. There was shooting down below as the men pursued the escaped prisoner. There was chaos around him. And then, through the fog and the snow, Chris Dolan saw a horrendous sight. An Indian leapt through the branches of a tree. His arms and legs were spread so wide, that Chris Dolan at first believed the man was flying. With a terrible whoop, he came down on a soldier – it was one of the men who'd been going to try to get around behind the escaped prisoner.

The Indian thrashed with a hatchet, opening vicious gashes across the soldier's face and chest.

And then there were Indians everywhere around them. Some shot muskets. Others jabbed with spears or slashed with hatchets.

Chris Dolan felt the weight of his Colt Navy in his hand. Without much thought, he raised the gun, drew back the hammer, and fired a shot into an Indian. He saw through the smoke that a hole opened up in the man's chest, but the man was still coming. Dolan cocked the hammer and fired another shot, and the Indian ran full into him.

Both men fell to the ground, and Dolan shouted and kicked and threw his fists, and then he realized that the Indian wasn't moving. His eyes were open, looking into the fog in the tops of the trees, but the man was dead.

Craig Dolan grabbed his little brother by the arm and jerked him to his feet.

"Retreat to the horses," Craig Dolan said to his brother. In all the chaos, Craig seemed to be calm, and his influence on his younger brother also calmed Chris.

Another burst of gunfire came from down below the ridge line. Chris did not know if it was soldiers shooting at Moses Calhoun or if it was soldiers shooting at Indians.

Chris Dolan stumbled back toward the horses. Several men were also retreating to the horses.

Sergeant Terry was there, and Lieutenant Fisher. They were shouting orders, attempting to repulse the Indian attack.

And as he watched, Dolan saw the Snake warriors vanish back into the fog, back into the spruce branches.

A dead calm seemed to descend upon the trail and the soldiers there.

A man moaned, and another man cried out for help.

"Were they with Calhoun?" Lieutenant Fisher asked.

"I don't think so," Chris Dolan said. He was as close to anyone to the western side of the trail when the Indians launched their attack on the soldiers. Dolan's instinct, for that was all that it was, when he saw the first

Indian leap through the spruce branches and fall upon one of his fellow soldiers, was that the Indians had been nearby and launched their attack when they heard the shooting. He couldn't prove that, but it was the way it seemed to him at the time that it happened.

"Where did they come from?" Sergeant Terry demanded.

"Right up out of the mist," one of the soldiers said.

"Have they gone? Are they coming back?" Lieutenant Fisher asked.

No one had an answer, but more soldiers were now retreating back to horses. Some were stopping to help the wounded. For all the violence, there seemed to be relatively few men down.

Chris Dolan had seen the first man killed. His body so hacked that the man was barely recognizable. Another man was run through by a spear, the spear still sticking up out of his gut. He had propped himself against a tree trunk, but no one who saw him thought he would live through the afternoon.

Two other men had bad gashes – knife or hatchet wounds.

Others had superficial wounds, barely more than scratches, possibly inflicted by Indian weapons and possibly accidents.

After the confusion died down, they found one more soldier, farther down the slope, shot in the thigh. He had bled heavily and died from the blood loss.

Bearclaw Jim, of course, was also among the wounded. Someone had tied a bandage around the stumps on his hand. Chris Dolan was impressed to see how tough the old scout was. He wasn't moaning about the pain or even complaining about the loss of his digits. But he was vowing revenge.

"I don't care what it takes, I'll be wearing that sonuvabitch's hair on my belt before I leave out of these mountains."

A burial party used their knives to dig shallow graves for the dead. The wounded were bandaged.

Nothing could be done for the man with the spear through his gut.

While the burial party was working, Chris Dolan was standing nearby the man, unable to look at him. It was grotesque. He'd weeped, he'd shouted, he'd prayed. A couple of his close friends kneeled close to him and were talking to him.

"You boys walk away over there," Dolan heard him say.

The men did not argue. They stepped away, over close to where Dolan was standing. Dolan started to ask what was going on, but then he heard the gunshot and understood.

"Dig another grave," Sergeant Terry called to the burial party.

- 18 -

As the horses descended down out of the draw and out of the forest, they went into a gallop, bounding hard and fast over the open meadow.

The snow was collecting on the ground at a rapid pace, and the horses kicked up white clumps of it as they ran.

But they could only keep up the pace for a short distance. Moses Calhoun preferred this sorrel gelding not because he was fast but because he was sure-footed. At last they reined in, and Calhoun twisted in his saddle and looked behind him. He saw nothing of the soldiers giving pursuit.

The ponies seemed able to keep going at a run, but Calhoun decided it was better now to preserve all the energy they could.

"We'll keep going," he said. "Maybe even keep riding after dark. We've got to make that pass. As long as we're in this valley, we're easy prey."

If it was hard to see in the woods and up on the trail, it was worse down in the meadow. The snow was falling so hard and fast here that it was like a lace veil laid atop another lace veil. The gray mist mingled with the snow, so it was like looking through a couple of lace veils in the gloaming, those last vestiges of diminishing light at the end of the day.

They rode into the falling snow without talking, and the snow seemed to put all the riders in a trance.

The young boys were starting to get grumpy. The excitement of adventure had left them, and they were cold and hungry. Aka Ne'ai hushed them sharply. She was a tough woman, like her father, and she intended to raise tough boys.

They kept going well into the afternoon. The sight of the falling snow and the dark fog hanging in the air increased the feeling of the cold. The cold seemed to reach through their clothes, through their skin, and clutch at them on the inside. The cold seemed absolute, as if every place on earth was frozen and piled in snow.

The boys complained some more.

Aka Ne'ai spoke to them, and they both pulled their blankets tighter around them, but that had little effect.

The small party rode on, and the boys continued to complain.

"What's the matter with them?" Calhoun finally asked, for all of their complaints were made in a language he did not speak.

"They are cold," Aka Ne'ai explained. "And hungry. But more cold."

Calhoun looked at them, judging their size. They were young and small, both of them, and the ponies they rode were stout enough. The pony the older boy rode seemed a little stronger.

He reined in and dropped down off the sorrel. Aka Ne'ai and the boys also pulled their ponies to a halt.

Calhoun got his heavy bearskin coat. He'd been thinking about putting it on himself, and he hesitated for just a moment, trying to decide if the coat meant comfort or survival. For now, he decided, it merely meant comfort.

"Tell them both to get on the older one's pony," Calhoun said, and as Aka Ne'ai spoke, he walked over and lifted the younger boy from his pony and carried him to his older brother's pony. He sat the younger boy on the blanket in front of his older brother. Then Calhoun wrapped his bearskin coat around both boys, leaving an opening so that the older boy could reach around his brother and hold the bridle.

Calhoun used a length of rope to belt the coat around the boys.

"That will help," he said.

Aka Ne'ai closed her eyes and offered him a small bow of her head.

"Thank you," she said.

Moses Calhoun tied a lead from the other pony's war bridle and gave it to Aka Ne'ai.

"If the soldiers come again, and we have to run, let go of the lead," he said. "Leave the pony to save yourself."

"Will they follow us?" she asked.

"Of course they will," Moses Calhoun said.

"Even with the warriors there to fight them?"

"What?" Calhoun asked. "What warriors?"

"The Snake men," she said.

Calhoun stared at the woman with confusion on his furrowed brows. Aka Ne'ai stared back, just as confused.

"Did you not see them?" she asked.

"I only saw the white soldiers," Calhoun said.

"When we rode away, down to the –" she couldn't come up with the word.

"Down to the draw?" Calhoun asked.

"Yes. The draw. When we rode down to the draw, I saw them in the trees along the trail. They watched me and let me pass."

"Was your husband with them?" Calhoun asked.

"I did not see him. I do not think he was with them, but he would not have showed himself to me if he was. They were preparing to fight the white soldiers."

Calhoun nodded.

"To help us escape," he said.

Aka Ne'ai shook her head. "I do not think so."

"Then what else would they have been doing?"

Aka Ne'ai thought for a moment, trying to find all the words. Speaking a lot of English did not come easily to her anymore.

"They come for you, Tekaiten Toi-yah'-to'-ko. They think you have led the white soldiers to us, and so they come for your hair."

"But they just saw me fighting the white soldiers," he said.

Aka Ne'ai shrugged her shoulders.

"These are young men who want to fight," she said. "Our people have been running from the white soldiers and from the white house-people and from the white earth diggers. The white men are chasing away all the game and killing the buffalo and taking our land. So we run to other land looking for game that is plentiful. But some of the warriors are tired of running. And they only think of taking hair. They attack the wagon-people and steal from the house-people. And now they want your hair for bringing the white soldiers to us."

Calhoun took a long look on their back trail. There was nothing to be seen but the falling snow. Even the surrounding mountains were mere shapes of darkness against the snow and fog. The meadow stretched white for a seeming eternity.

"Will they keep coming now that they have fought the white soldiers?"

Aka Ne'ai shrugged.

"Maybe," she said. "For some, it would be a great victory to have the hair of Tekaiten Toi-yah'-to'-ko."

Moses Calhoun walked back over to the sorrel and

rubbed the horse's neck.

The soldiers were plenty to worry about. They had obviously decided that losing a prisoner was too much of an embarrassment and were determined to recapture him – or, more likely, execute him. But now he also had to worry about Indians chasing his scalp.

He stepped into the stirrup and swung himself up into the saddle.

"Let's make tracks," he said.

They rode on at a walk for some distance. The thick, falling snow mesmerizing to them. The boys, now, had stopped their complaints. They were almost thoroughly covered in the bearskin coat, and sitting together on the same pony also helped to keep them warm. A couple of times, the boys even giggled at each other.

Though Aka Ne'ai did not seem worried, she twisted around to look back several times, scanning the darkness for any sign of soldiers or Indians.

Late in the afternoon, about the time Moses Calhoun first thought he could see a shadow shape of the mountains ahead of them, Aka Ne'ai twisted to look back. She squinted hard into the white darkness behind them and gave a sharp intake of breath.

"What is it?" Calhoun said, looking at her.

"Something is behind us," she said.

Moses Calhoun twisted and looked back. He saw it, too. But it was neither the soldiers or Indians.

"It's that damned mule," he said with a chuckle of disbelief. "Stubborn to his core."

Calhoun thought of the provisions in the pannier and what those would mean to their chance for survival, but he also thought of that damned mule. Any mule that would catch up to horses that had charged at a gallop through a snow-drenched meadow was a mule worth having.

"Keep going," he said. "I'll catch back up. I'm going to catch that stubborn mule."

***

Late in the day it had become almost impossible to distinguish the dusk of evening from the dark of night. Mercifully, the snow had stopped an hour or so before, but the fog and gray darkness persisted.

Though Moses Calhoun desperately wanted to reach the pass where he believed they might find safety, he decided they had to spare the horses and themselves.

He led his little group of refugees across the meadow and into the forest of spruce trees.

"Tell the boys to keep their heads down," Calhoun said, stepping out of his saddle. "You and I will have to walk from here, but they can stay on their pony."

Calhoun led his sorrel horse, the mule, and the younger boy's pony. Aka Ne'ai led her pony and the boys' pony.

They crunched through the snow on the outskirts of the tree line until Calhoun found a spot where they could enter the trees. It was just a deer path, but it was a path into the woods. He had no way of judging if the path would grow too steep or if they would be able to get deeper into the woods. But the path cut and twisted along fairly level, and they soon found themselves deeper into the woods and staring at a tall, vertical rock face. Calhoun looked up it, but the top of the rocky cliff was lost in the fog and coming of night.

"We'll camp here," he said. "We'll make for the pass first thing in the morning."

Aka Ne'ai got her children down from the pony and helped Calhoun to stake the animals in the small clearing at the base of the cliff.

"Have the boys collect any dry wood they can find," Calhoun said. "We'll bury a fire so it can't be seen, and just pray that no one passes near enough to smell it."

While the boys collected wood, Calhoun cut several fresh spruce boughs and fashioned a lean-to shelter against a low, sturdy pine branch.

The snow had fallen hard enough that it lay in thick patches all over the woods, but there were spaces beneath the trees that, while wet, were clear of snow. Aka Ne'ai gathered pine straw and put it down on the floor of the shelter.

Calhoun used his Bowie knife to dig out a hole for the fire. He built it near the shelter opening so that any warmth it gave off might be caught inside and give comfort to them overnight.

At last, Calhoun used flint to spark some dry pine straw he had twisted together. When the twist of pine straw caught, he blew on it softly, pushing it down under a small teepee of twigs he had erected at the cusp of the hole he'd dug. As those twigs started to catch fire, Calhoun put some larger sticks down. When those caught, he gently pushed the fire down into the hole.

The hole was not so deep, but it was deep enough that if he was careful about how much wood he put on the fire it would prevent anyone from seeing the flames through the forest.

There was nothing he could do about the scent of the smoke, though he hoped the heavy mist would hold the smoke close to campsite.

With the fire going and the boys huddled under a blanket inside the small shelter, Calhoun put on his bearskin coat. It was some relief against the cold, and the fire helped, too.

He cooked a meal of biscuits and venison and made coffee – all things he would not have been able to do if that mule hadn't followed them.

After they had eaten, the children and Aka Ne'ai slept in the shelter.

Moses Calhoun sat with his back leaning against the trunk of the pine tree he had used to build the shelter. He stretched his legs out toward the fire. He loaded and primed his rifle and laid it across his lap. Though he had the heavy bearskin coat around him, he pulled a blanket up over him, too.

His feet were cold and wet. He would have liked to take off his boots and socks and dry them by the fire, but he did not dare. He knew too well that disaster and violence could fall upon them at any moment, and he was not going to be caught with his boots off.

He dozed some, but mostly stayed awake through the night, propped against the pine tree.

He listened to the sounds of the forest.

An owl screeched in the distance. A wolf somewhere far away howled. Snow-laden branches, bent under the weight, released their burden and the snow fell like thunder through the branches to land on the ground. Some branches, weak from age or disease, gave a sharp snap and collapsed with the snow.

He thought of Kee Kuttai, warm in their cabin with Daniel and Elijah. Probably by now they were all bedded down in the loft, in that space where the heat from the fire collected and offered a cozy retreat from the cold of the day. He'd have given anything to be home.

Moses Calhoun had gone on many long winter hunts. Spending a night in the forest with snow all around him was a comfort of its own. There was a familiarity to it. But this was different, of course. There were always dangers, but those dangers came from animals or, less likely, an attack by a small band of rogue Indians or, even less likely, white outlaws who might have sought escape in the mountains. But never before had Moses found himself hunted by white soldiers and Indian warriors alike.

It was a damned uncomfortable position.

Calhoun's eyes snapped open and he tried to judge if he'd been asleep or simply dozing.

A gray light permeated around him, and he knew dawn was breaking out in the meadow. The fog was so thick, Calhoun thought he might have to use his hatchet to cut his way out of it.

Had it been an owl or a man he heard scream?

That's what woke him. A shout or a scream.

And then he heard the snap of a pistol. And then another. And then he heard the high-pitched, undulating howl of an Indian charging to battle. And more pistol shots.

"What is it?" Aka Ne'ai asked, waking at the sound of the shooting.

"A fight," Calhoun said. "Probably out in the meadow, and not terribly far from us right now."

"What do we do?" she asked.

Calhoun listened. It was getting hotter now. More shouting. More war whoops. More shooting.

The man's memory was like a map of these mountains, and he called to mind now his memories of the places he had been, the times he had come through the mountain pass down into this valley, the times he had tracked elk away from the pass, through the forest.

"I do not think we can make the pass," Calhoun said. "Whoever wins that battle will stay there, probably all morning. Collecting trophies and burying their dead. If the snow resumes this morning or if it's fallen overnight, the pass might be so deep by the time we get there that we'll not make it through, not quickly enough to escape whoever might be left to pursue us."

"What will we do?" Aka Ne'ai asked, and Moses Calhoun could hear in her voice a tone of fear.

"There's other ways," Calhoun said.

"But if we can't get through the pass, maybe the soldiers will not be able to get through the pass and will not come to the village," Aka Ne'ai said.

"No, the soldiers will get through," Calhoun said. "It's not impassible. The snow would slow us, and give an opportunity to anyone who might be chasing us – whether that's your people or the white soldiers. Either way, we've got to get moving."

The boys offered no complaint about not getting

breakfast, accustomed as they were to lean times.

Calhoun again put them both on one pony and bundled them in his heavy coat.

And within minutes, the small party was off again, riding along the cliff face until Calhoun saw a tree-lined draw. The ridges on either side of it were too steep to mount, but the draw rose steadily to higher ground, and Calhoun decided to chance it. Features in the terrain tended to do the same things. Most draws on the side of a mountain would rise to meet a ridge where a natural trail would form. So Calhoun took the chance that the draw would get them higher, take them closer to a place where he might find a path that would take them around the mountain and on to the other side.

He kept the sorrel moving. Calhoun understood that this was a long-distance race, and if he was going to win out over the soldiers, or the Indians, he might need a horse with energy to spare. So even as they could hear the gun battle behind them, he set off on foot, leading his party of refugees up the mountain and away from the pass, away from the closest opportunity for escape.

- 19 -

The Indian warriors attacked at the first light of dawn.

They came out of the fog like wraiths, charging into the camp the soldiers had erected on the edge of the tree line.

The charge was more horrible than the one on the trail, at least Chris Dolan believed it was.

All night he had been awake. Every time he shut his eyes to try for sleep, Dolan's mind was filled with a vision of the Indian who had come through the spruce boughs like a hawk swooping down on its prey. His face – the face Private Dolan saw in his imagination – was something terrible, something unearthly, painted and hideous and fearsome.

That face haunted Dolan through the night so that by the time the first light of dawn showed, the young cavalry volunteer was so exhausted and filled with fright that he thought he would never sleep again.

And now, when the young soldier believed the light of morning was bringing safety, the face that haunted his imagination was back, and multiplied, and renewing its dreadful attack.

The Indians rushed into the camp, coming at the run, slashing with their hatchets and knives, stabbing with their spears.

Chris Dolan was lying on a blanket with it doubled over and wrapped around him. Now he rolled, wrestling to get himself free, forgetting his brace of revolvers. Hands and knees, he scrambled to get away, running for the woods and thinking he might find safety there. Now he was up on his feet, crouched, but running.

Arrows sailed through the camp.

Men were screaming. Dolan's fellow soldiers.

A few tried to fight back. A couple of revolvers sounded behind him, and then a couple of more. Others were running, like Chris Dolan, toward the woods, hoping to find safety there.

The Indians shouted a terrible war whoop. They grabbed the soldiers, relishing the hand-to-hand fighting. Dolan looked back over his shoulder. He saw two Indians wrestling one soldier to the ground. The soldier had an arrow sticking out of his ribs. One Indian warrior held the man's arm, pinned to the ground. The other Indian straddled his chest. He took out a knife and grabbed at the man's hair.

Chris Dolan looked away.

He turned the other direction, trying to find his brother Craig or Hep Chandler.

He saw Billy Douglas.

Billy.

He had a hatchet in his back. An Indian swung a fist and hit Billy in the back of the head. Billy, who was trying to get away, dropped to the ground. The Indian planted a foot on Billy's back and yanked at the hatchet until it broke free. Then he swung it down hard, opening the back of Billy's head like a watermelon.

Chris Dolan heard a sob of horror, and realized it had come from him.

Lieutenant Fisher was trying to rally the men, calling to them with his saber raised.

An Indian charged him, and Fisher swung down with the saber, slicing the man from his shoulder blade to his hip bone.

But then there was a rush of men, three or four of them on Lieutenant Fisher. He swung with his saber, but someone grabbed his arm. The last Chris Dolan saw of Lieutenant Fisher, the officer was on the ground and it seemed like eight or ten men were on top of him, going at him with knives and slashing away bits of his uniform.

Chris Dolan made the trees. He just started to push back a branch so that he could get inside the tree line and, he prayed, find safety in the woods. And then he felt an almighty push from behind and he tumbled forward, face-first through the branches.

Someone fell on top of him, and Chris tried to roll, tried to at least get off his stomach so that he could fight back.

And just by his ear, a deafening shot from a revolver that rattled his head and deafened him.

And then the man on his back was up and hands were clutching at him, dragging him to his feet.

"We've got to run, Chris," a voice shouted at him.

Chris looked around. It was Craig and Hep Chandler with him, Hep pointing his gun through the spruce branches, Craig dragging him deeper into the woods.

And then all three of them were running, darting through the forest, jumping fallen trees and stumps, ducking under branches, hopping over small saplings.

The three men ran as hard as they could. Behind them, the horrible sounds of battle continued. The Indian shouts froze the blood in their veins.

As they ran, they heard others crashing through the woods.

Hep Chandler turned to shoot and realized that the Lakota scout and Bearclaw Jim were also sprinting through the woods.

They jumped down into a gully, the two brothers and Hep Chandler. All three of them misjudged the depth of the gully – it was eight feet to the bottom – and they landed hard and fell to the ground. They all got up brushing themselves off. Hep Chandler uncocked his revolver, swept by relief that he'd not had his finger on the trigger when he tumbled into the bottom of the gully.

"I might have shot one of you," he breathed. "Or

myself."

Between them, they had four guns, both Hep and Craig had grabbed their Colts; one box of spare balls and percussion caps, only Craig thought he might need to reload; and two coats. Thankfully, all three men were wearing their boots when their camp was overrun.

"It's a rout," Craig Dolan said.

The three men spoke in hushed tones.

"They killed Billy," Chris said.

Hep Chandler held his side, pressing against a stitch. Hep didn't even have his coat on. He'd slept with his coat draped over him, and when he rolled from his blanket to get up and fight, he grabbed his saddle holsters, but not his coat. But he did not yet even feel the cold.

"I saw the sergeant," Hep said. "He was riding with a couple of the boys toward the pass."

"Running from the fight?" Chris asked.

"Don't say nothing about it," Craig said, his jaw clenched. "We ran from the fight, too."

"Yeah," Chris said. "But I wouldn't have expected it of the sergeant."

"The lieutenant was killed," Craig said.

"I saw it," Chris said.

"We've got to keep going," Hep Chandler said.

But then they heard movement in the woods above them, and by instinct all three pressed themselves against the earth, trying to hide in the gully.

They waited until the noise trailed off.

Chris Dolan thought he'd held his breath for ten

minutes.

"What do we do?" Chris asked, his voice the softest of whispers.

"Give me a boost up," Craig said.

Chris cupped his hands and his brother stepped into his hands like he was stepping into a stirrup. Chris raised his brother just high enough that Craig Dolan could see over the edge of the gulley.

"Nobody's up there," he said, coming back down. He looked along the gulley and saw where it was not nearly as deep just a little ways beyond where they stood. "Let's go up this away and go out the other side. We'll put distance between us and the slaughter."

The sound of gunfire had diminished now, but they could hear yelling. They tried not to listen so well as to determine if the shouting they heard was the screams of their fellow soldiers or the victory cries of the Indians.

As they came up out of the gulley, they saw another blue-coated soldier running through the woods. It was Matthew Dorsey, and he looked scared and confused.

"Matty!" Chris called to him, and Chris started to run to the man.

Craig Dolan reached out to grab his brother, to stop him, but Chris was already gone.

"Damnation," Craig said, running after Chris.

Chris Dolan caught up to Matthew Dorsey and grabbed him by the arm, spinning the man around.

Dorsey's eyes seemed far distant, unfocused.

"Matty," Chris said. "It's me. Chris."

Then Chris looked down and saw that Dorsey was

shot through the stomach by an arrow. And he had another protruding from the back of his shoulder. Both were buried deep in him, the ends protruding from his body, though, were short, broken off as he ran through the woods and crashed into branches.

"Injuns," Matt Dorsey said.

Chris nodded at him. "It's okay. We're going to get out of here."

As he said it, Chris heard a movement off to his side, and he looked to see an Indian let loose an arrow. This one hit Matthew Dorsey in the side, and he stumbled forward into Chris.

And then the Indian was charging at Chris, coming on with a hatchet raised up high over his head.

Chris had to push Matthew off of him, and he staggered backwards, raising up his hands to try to protect himself, but he was too late. The hatchet was coming down at him, the Indian's face a cruel snarl as he let out a fierce shriek.

The hatchet felt like nothing more than a punch to his chest. The pain he expected wasn't there. At least not right away.

Chris couldn't think fast enough to react. The Indian raised up the hatchet again, and Chris tried to cover his face with his arms.

Then he heard the snap of the pistol.

He saw the Indian reel. The pistol cracked again, the shot destroying the man's head.

Chris turned and saw Hep Chandler holding a smoking revolver.

Craig grabbed Chris by the arms.

"How bad are you hurt?"

Still thinking he'd not had any more than a punch to the chest, Chris shook his head.

"Not bad," he said.

But his older brother was looking at his chest. Craig was pale, the look in his eyes horrified. When Chris looked down his knees went weak. He had an enormous gash across his chest, leaking blood all over his ripped coat.

The pain came like a giant wave, washing over Chris. His knees got weak and he started to go down, but Craig took him under one arm, and Hep Chandler under the other.

"Hold on little brother," Craig said.

They went on either side of Chris, supporting him and moving as quickly as they could through the woods, fearful that others of the Indian warriors might have heard their shots and could be coming.

They went deeper into the woods, and started up the slope. There was no trail, so they had to make their way incrementally, five- or ten-yards at a time. Craig Dolan and Hep Chandler struggled against the weight of Craig's younger brother, who did what he could but felt weak and dizzy.

Several times they had to stop and catch their breath. During one of their breaks, Craig took his belt and buckled it tight around Chris's blood-soaked coat, hoping at least to do something to put pressure on the wound and hold it closed.

They found themselves at the base of a rocky cliff, and worked their way around it until they found a narrow fissure that they could climb.

The incline was rough. They had to stop several times to catch their breath. It was not hand-over-hand climbing, but in places they did have to do the work on their hands and knees. Any one of the men might have made it on his own without so much difficulty, but the two men pushing and pulling the wounded man made the work more difficult. On rocky ledges they peered out, looking through the canopy of the spruce trees, searching the fog – seeking either survivors or pursuers. But they saw neither.

Craig Dolan and Hep Chandler thought only of immediate survival. Escaping the Indians.

They did not consider what they might do come nightfall – not how they would replenish the energy they burned on the long climb nor how they would keep warm. All that mattered, now, was getting away from the men who had slaughtered their patrol.

The three men came out on top of the rocky cliff, and in front of them the mountain stretched higher, the forest of pine and spruce seemed to go on forever. The slope was steep, but not impossible if they kept going at an angle, around the mountain rather than trying to climb over it.

"They won't follow us," Hep Chandler said, not certain of it himself.

"We ain't safe," Craig Dolan said. "We've got to keep moving. We won't be safe until we find the regiment."

Craig looked at Chris. The boy was pale and weak, and there was so much blood soaked into his coat.

"Can you make it, Chris?" Craig said. "We've got to keep going."

"I can make it," Chris said weakly.

Craig and Hep glanced at each other.

"We've just got to keep him moving," Hep said.

The three men continued to move, finding a ridge that pushed them higher up the mountain, but also taking them around toward the south. The trees here were not as thick as they were below, and in those spaces where there were small clearings, the snow had piled thick.

The trudged on, though, through snow, over boulders, under branches.

After an hour or more of walking, Chris Dolan finally collapsed.

Craig and Hep fell with him, too exhausted to keep moving. Hep Chandler felt frozen. In their exertion, they had broken a sweat, despite the cold, and now the sweat seemed to freeze. He's whole body felt like ice.

"Rest for a few minutes," Craig said. "But we can't stay here. We'll die on this mountain if we stay here."

The men caught their breath. Chris Dolan started to slip off to sleep, but Craig patted his face and spoke to him, keeping him awake.

"We're going to get you out of here," Craig said.

Then somewhere from down below them on the trail, but not far away, they heard movement in the trees. A horse blew.

And Craig Dolan, desperate to keep his brother alive, froze with fear.

- 20 -

Moses Calhoun drew the reins on his horse and held out a hand to signal to Aka Ne'ai and the children to stop.

He'd seen something through the fog up ahead, some movement.

The sorrel gelding let out a heavy blow and shook his head. Calhoun swung a leg over the horse's rump and stepped down out of his saddle. He slid his hatchet from his belt and started to move forward along the ridge. It did not take long for him to find what he'd seen.

Three soldiers, one in just his shirt and one who

appeared to be badly wounded. It was clear enough what had happened. Calhoun had gone a wide route, up through the draw, and circled back around. These men had found a tight space to make a direct ascent, and they'd come out in front of him.

Two of the soldiers were pointing revolvers in his direction.

Calhoun slid the hatchet back into his belt. Three men on a mountainside, lost, cold, and hurt. Even with their revolvers in their fists, these men were no threat to him.

"Lower them guns," Calhoun said, stepping toward them. "I ain't your enemy."

The two men did what he told them to do, both of them lowering the hammers on their revolvers. Calhoun continued walking toward them and then realized that the three men had been his guards.

"He's hurt bad," one said, nodding to the injured man.

"That's Christopher, ain't it," Calhoun said, stepping to the wounded man and kneeling down beside him.

"That's right. Chris," Craig said. "I'm Craig. That's Hep."

Moses Calhoun unbuckled the belt and opened the ripped coat so that he could see the wound. It was a deep gash across the boy's chest, and it had bled something fierce. But Moses Calhoun had seen worse.

"If we can get him off this mountain, he'll be telling folks for years to come how he got that scar across his chest," Calhoun said.

Somehow the man's words brought comfort to Craig

Dolan, who was near to giving up on his brother.

"Are you sure?"

Calhoun shrugged.

"Nothing's certain on this earth," he said. "Small enough chance of getting off this mountain. But the wound itself ain't fatal. We need to get him bandaged, and we need to keep moving."

He looked over Craig and Hep Chandler.

"You're the one I'm more worried about," he said, pointing a gloved finger at Hep Chandler. "What in hell are you doing out here in just a shirt, son?"

"Freezing," Hep Chandler said.

Calhoun looked at the three men and glanced back to his charges on the ponies. He already had more responsibility on this mountain than he cared for.

"Hand over them guns," Calhoun said. "And I'll do what I can for you."

"Like hell," Craig Dolan said.

"Then you're on your own," Calhoun said, and he stood up and started back toward his horse. "If you try to stop us from passing, I'll finish what them Snake warriors started."

"Wait!" Craig said. "You can't leave us. My brother's hurt bad."

Calhoun continued to his horse and took up the reins, pulling his horse up the trail to walk past the three soldiers.

"He is hurt bad," Calhoun said. "And you boys have worked yourselves into a rough patch here. But I ain't helping men who have been chasing me and won't hand over their weapons to me."

It was the cold that got to Hep Chandler.

"We'll give you our guns," he said. "Give him your guns, Craig."

Calhoun stopped, trying to decide.

He wasn't bluffing when he offered to leave the men, and he wasn't inclined now to accept the guns and stay and help them. But he knew two of these men would be dead by morning without him, and the third probably wouldn't make it back to his regiment.

Calhoun looked around to Aka Ne'ai. Her face was impassive. She seemed indifferent to helping or not helping, going forward or staying put. The two boys were wrapped again in Calhoun's bearskin coat. One pony had no rider.

"Quickly," Calhoun said. "We don't know who might be below us coming on in pursuit. Set them guns down and help me."

First Calhoun found in his pannier some rolled strips of bandages he carried with him. He had them in case his horse turned an ankle or he turned an ankle or he had to patch himself up after a bear or lion attack. He had a tin of salve. It was a mixture of honey and crushed goldenrod.

"Take off his coat and shirt," Calhoun said. "Use some snow from over there to clean the wound off. Then put a layer of this on it."

He handed the tin to Craig Dolan.

"Wrap his chest tight in these," he said, handing the rolled bandages to Hep Chandler. "Make sure it's tight."

The two men did what Calhoun told them to, and

while they treated the injured soldier, Calhoun took two blankets and cut holes in the center of them. It wasn't much, but they would serve as coats for Hep Chandler and Chris Dolan. He hated to destroy the blankets, particularly as they were the only blankets he had.

Chris Dolan came in and out of consciousness. The boy needed something to get his strength back, but they could not take the time now to make him food.

"Give him some water from my canteen," Calhoun said.

While they tended to the wounded soldier, Moses Calhoun listened for any sound from below. He had little doubt that the Indians would be coming, if not for him then surely for the three soldiers. Those Snake warriors wanted every white scalp they could lay hands on.

When at last they had done the things Calhoun told them to, and wrapped Chris in the blanket that Calhoun had turned into a poncho, the three men lifted him onto the pony.

"You'll have to walk along beside him and keep him on the pony, but it'll be a sight better than trying to tote him on your shoulders," Calhoun said.

Calhoun took the two gunbelts with the four pistols and stowed them in the mule's pack. The soldiers, if they were so inclined, could retrieve their gunbelts as they walked behind Calhoun, but he didn't think they would try it. Those men were desperate to survive the afternoon, and Calhoun knew as well as they did that he was their one hope.

Now they resumed their climb along the ridge, higher up the mountain on a trail that Calhoun hoped would take them around to the east side of the mountain where they would have a chance to get to safety.

***

Sergeant Terry made the pass with two of his soldiers late in the afternoon. They snow had resumed in the morning, and it was now so heavy that a man could not see fifty feet in front of him.

The soldiers had to dismount. The snow was piled so deep that it wasn't safe to ride. Each man went ahead of his horse to be sure there were no holes or deep crevices that might cause a horse to throw a rider or worse, break a leg.

Sergeant Terry didn't go ten steps without looking back over his shoulder.

Neither the sergeant nor the two men with him had uttered an unnecessary word. They didn't speak of the horror they fled. They didn't talk about the lieutenant's death, or the men they saw hacked down all around them. Each of the three men escaped on his own, but they all fled the same way. They were lucky, all three of them. When the attack came, they were already in the process of saddling their horses. They weren't alone. There was a half dozen other men likewise engaged, men who were eager to get to the pass and back to the regiment. But those others, the ones who didn't make it, they rushed back to help their fellow soldier.

Sergeant Terry threw a leg over the saddle and began whipping his horse with his reins.

The others saw him escape and followed his lead.

And now just the three of them had made the pass.

"You think anyone else survived, Sergeant?" one of the men asked. Sergeant Terry glanced at him. He was a young man, maybe not but eighteen or nineteen years old. One of the youngest in a patrol full of mostly young man. The boy's voice sounded full of fear, and he had a faraway look in his eyes.

"No telling," Sergeant Terry said.

"I saw some of the boys run for the woods. Them two scouts went for the woods."

Terry grunted but did not respond.

The other man spoke up now. Though he was a volunteer, like most all the others, he was also an experienced man. He'd come from California, but he'd prospected with a small outfit in the Sierra Nevada mountains. He'd seen bear and heavy snow.

"I'll tell you this much," he said. "Anyone who survived but didn't make this pass won't live through the night."

Sergeant Terry's horse had come to a standstill and was refusing to move. The man turned his back to the east and heaved with all his might to get the horse to take a step.

"What makes you think that we're going to live through the night?" Sergeant Terry said. "You think we're so lucky just because we got away? Them Injuns will be after us. And if they don't get us, the cold will."

The other man, the one who'd prospected in the Sierra Nevada, he shook his head.

"No, sir, Sergeant," he said with a grin. "We might have to worry about the cold and the snow, but them Injuns is done with us."

"How do you reckon?" Terry asked.

"I saw them," he said. "When they saw that Injun scout with us, they were more interested in him than they was us."

Sergeant Terry had the horse going now and was facing east again, but he turned and checked over his shoulder. He did not believe the Indians were done with them.

"If you're right, and they go after Jack Cut Face and Bearclaw Jim, we can consider ourselves lucky for that," Sergeant Terry said. "Of course, once we're through this pass, I don't know how we find the regiment without one of the two of them."

The other man, spoke up again, and his voice sounded hollow.

"It was terrible," he said. "They hacked up all our men."

- 21 -

"Three ponies and a horse," the Lakota scout said, studying the tracks in the wet dirt. "Three men on foot."

Bearclaw Jim chewed his lip.

"You figure it's that man Calhoun?"

Jack Cut Face nodded, a severe look on his face. Of course, with that scar he could not do much to alter the severe look on his face.

"It's the white hunter," Jack Cut Face said.

"He's picked up some pilgrims," Bearclaw Jim said.

"What you reckon?"

"Does he have a wife and children with the Snake tribe?" the Lakota asked.

"Beats me if he does," Bearclaw Jim said.

The Lakota scout stood up and looked around at all of the muddy prints.

"Two soldiers are with him," he said. "Maybe three."

The two men had found the bloodied coat and shirt of one of the soldiers on the trail back behind them. They'd been expecting to find a body, but still had not. Now, finding the tracks, Bearclaw Jim began to wonder if Moses Calhoun had stumbled into the soldiers and gotten himself taken hostage. More likely, he came upon the soldiers and offered to help them. That's what it looked like. Whoever else was with Calhoun – likely Snake Indians on ponies – it looked like Calhoun was leading at the front of this group.

"How far up ahead?" Bearclaw Jim asked.

The Lakota shrugged.

"I cannot say."

"Well, I'll tell you this much, I'd like to pay that sonuvabitch back for what he done to my hand. I guess I wouldn't mind too much getting that horse and them ponies, neither."

"We can catch him," the Lakota scout said. "But we have to worry that those Snake bastards catch us up from behind."

"Then let's keep moving," Bearclaw Jim said.

The two men had little opportunity to get provisions. Like the other survivors, they fled by running. Bearclaw

Jim had his possibles bag slung over his shoulder, and his Lancaster rifle, for all the good it did him. The man couldn't shoot with his thumb and trigger finger blown off. The Lakota had a musket, and both men had knives.

At least they were warm. Experienced in the mountains, they never shed their coats or boots, and when the Snake warriors attacked the soldiers' camp, both men were dressed to flee in a hurry.

"Sure would like to have a horse," Bearclaw Jim said as they made their way up the trail, occasionally spotting tracks in the mud or in patches of snow.

The ridge they followed broke free of the tree line, and the two men found themselves exposed to the heavy snowfall. They kept going, following the natural trail created by the ridge, and up ahead it reached a peak, and then the ridge dropped lower, back toward the tree line.

The heavy flakes seemed to be pouring from the sky, but at least here they were above the fog that still hung thick over the valley. As they reached the precipice of the ridge, where it started to drop down into the trees, the Lakota scout reached out a hand and took Bearclaw Jim by the arm. The older scout stopped and squinted through the snow. It took him a moment, but about a hundred yards ahead of them he saw the small group they had been following.

"Can you hit him from here?" Bearclaw Jim asked.

Jack Cut Face wasn't much of a hand with a gun. He carried a smooth bore musket, which did not help. He was better at fighting with his knife and his hands, and he could shoot a man at thirty yards with a bow and arrow. But his lack of ability with a gun had never registered with him. Like many men, Jack Cut Face did not know his own limitations.

"I can hit him," he said, already ramming a ball down the barrel of the musket.

"Don't shoot if you can't hit him," Bearclaw Jim said. "I'd rather keep going and get closer than let them know we're here."

"I can hit him," Jack Cut Face said again, bringing the musket up to his shoulder.

"Hell of a shot from this distance," Bearclaw Jim said.

Jack Cut Face squeezed the trigger. The flint fell and the powder ignited and the gun exploded. The ball sailed over the heads of the small party and crashed through the branches of the spruce trees ahead of them.

The lead man swung around. At this distance, Bearclaw Jim couldn't see his face, but he recognized Moses Calhoun by his clothes.

"Damn, you missed."

Calhoun was hurrying the others along the trail now. Encouraging them to get into the tree line.

Undaunted, Jack Cut Face was quickly trying to load another shot.

Bearclaw Jim started considered breaking into a run. He was hell in a close-up fight, and he figured that even with a shot-off hand he could still whip most men. But he heard a noise behind them, from somewhere lower down the mountain. It was a high-pitched, long yelp. And then an identical yelp answered it.

"B'god it's them Injuns coming behind us," Bearclaw Jim said.

He started to run again, but he saw that the mountain hunter was still standing in the same spot up ahead of them.

He'd let the others pass, and his horse and mule had passed, too. The others were all almost to the tree line. But the mountain hunter stood his ground. He had grabbed something from the pannier on the mule, and Bearclaw Jim now realized he had thrown one of the soldier's gunbelts over his shoulder, and he was standing armed with two Colt Navy revolvers.

"We're caught now," Bearclaw Jim said.

He could not see the Indians coming behind them, but he knew they were there. And he knew upon hearing the shot of the musket that they would be coming fast.

He looked at the steep, snow-covered slope below him.

"Nothing else for it," he said, and Bearclaw Jim crouched down and started to slide down the slope. The Lakota primed his pan and raised up his musket. He sent another useless shot flying into the spruce trees, though the second shot was a bit closer to its target. And then Jack Cut Face followed Bearclaw Jim down the steep slope.

By the time they reached the trees below them, both men's attempt at controlling their descent had turned to chaos as they tumbled head-over-heels. Bearclaw Jim crashed hard into a big lodgepole pine and laid in the wet pine straw breathing heavily. He'd dropped his Lancaster rifle, but it had slid down the slope to within a few yards of him.

Jack Cut Face managed himself slightly better. He slid to a stop in a pile of snow, gun still in hand.

The two men staggered to their feet. Bearclaw Jim retrieved his gun. Then they hurried under the cover of trees, now following Moses Calhoun and his small party, but well below them on the slope.

***

Moses Calhoun heard the war cry from the Indians and watched the two scouts disappear over the side of the ridge.

He waited, giving the others a chance to keep moving down the ridge some under the cover of the trees. He watched for the Indians. He would face them if he had to, and he would rather face them here on this ridge where he could see them coming. And he knew they were coming. Even if they'd been ready to abandon the chase, those two shots would encourage them to keep coming.

After several minutes still not seeing the pursuers, Calhoun gave up and hurried along the ridge under the trees, catching up to the others.

"What was it?" Craig Dolan asked.

"Your scouts," Calhoun said.

"Why would they shoot at us?" Dolan asked.

"I reckon because I shot Bearclaw Jim in the hand," Calhoun said.

Dolan nodded, remembering now.

"I suppose so," he said.

"We have bigger problems than those scouts," Calhoun said. "If they didn't know before, the Indians know now where we are. They're convinced I was scouting for the soldiers, and they're coming after me. If they find you with me, there won't be any convincing them otherwise."

Calhoun looked at young Chris Dolan on the pony. The boy was pale and could barely hold his eyes open. He was another worry.

Aka Ne'ai had taken the lead of the group when Calhoun stayed back to confront the two scouts. Now Moses Calhoun took the lead on his horse and cut a trail around some trees to get back in front of Aka Ne'ai.

He owed no allegiance to these white soldiers who, ultimately, were the reason he was even involved in all of this. All the same, he'd taken the three men in and offered them protection, and he did not now wish to see one of them die while in his care. But Chris Dolan needed to be cared for. He needed sustenance and warmth, more than anything.

They were following the natural trail made by the ridge, and their course made pursuit a simple thing, both for the Snake warriors and for the two army scouts. Calhoun wasn't surprised that the scout, Bearclaw Jim, was seeking him out. The soldiers said Calhoun's shot had amputated a finger and thumb, and that was the sort of thing that made a man thirsty for revenge.

As they went along, Calhoun studied the terrain of the mountain, looking for draws or ridges that dropped lower, a place where they might abandon their current path.

He needed to get under the cover of trees where he would be able to make shelter, have fuel for a fire, and find what he needed to tend to the injured soldier.

When they finally reached a place where the slope dropping from the side of the ridge was easier for the horses, Calhoun started down. They were less than thirty yards from the tree line. He wondered if he'd be able to see the Snake camp were it not for the heavy fog that had settled down in the valley.

The snow was still falling, coming down in large flakes and falling rapidly. Out here, exposed as they were on the ridge, the snow piled thick, and it was getting harder to walk through easily. But even when they managed to get down to the trees, the snow was starting to cover the ground, not just in patches now, but even under the tall pines and spruce the snow was falling off of branches and getting down to the ground.

There was no trail here now, and Calhoun had to pick his way through the forest, finding the places where the horse and mule and the ponies with their riders could pass. The tree branches presented one obstacle, and the undergrowth created another. Calhoun did his best to avoid deep snow where they would leave tracks that were easy to follow. But it meant slow-going.

They walked on for a long time, an hour, then another.

Little in the way of conversation passed.

The soldiers were lost. With the heavy cloud cover, even up on the ridge they had no idea where the sun was and they'd lost all sense of direction. They did not know if they were on the east or west face of the mountain. They did not know if they were walking south or north.

All they knew was one step in front of the next, and keep Chris Dolan from falling off the pony.

Aka Ne'ai also had little notion of where they were. What she knew, having been raised by old Eli Simmons, was that men like her father and men like Moses Calhoun tended to know where they were going and what they were doing.

And then there was a low rumble from somewhere up ahead.

"What's that noise?" Hep Chandler asked, and his voice – after so much quiet – sounded strange even to himself.

"It's a creek up ahead," Calhoun said. "It's the same water that borders the Snake camp."

Through this whole area there were several north-flowing rivers, a thing that continued to create havoc with this North Carolina native. Calhoun was accustomed to rivers that flowed south and east, mostly, and north flowing rivers still made him stop and think.

"Are we that near the Injun camp?" Hep asked. "You're not intending to take us there, are you?"

"We're not near it," Calhoun said. "That stream flows down through a canyon and makes a couple of big drops before it cuts out into the valley. The canyon ain't passable, neither. We'd have to follow the creek all the way down to the valley to cross it and get to the camp."

The rumble grew louder until they found themselves walking a high, wooded ridge looking down on the creek, probably a hundred feet or more below them.

The creek rushed over its rocky bottom, cutting through shoals, and making quite a racket. It was always dropping over short falls, but as they continued to walk upstream, they neared a place where the water dropped down a twenty-foot fall and the noise grew louder.

The horse didn't like the noise. His ears became rigid, and his nostrils swelled, and he kept shaking his head and looking at the water rushing below them.

The canyon below them made Calhoun nervous. If the Indians, or the scouts, caught them here, there was little opportunity for escape. But it could also provide them with the cover they needed. They were back down in the low fog now. The noise of the stream and the water fall would mask any noise the animals made.

At length, Calhoun found a spot that seemed good enough.

"We're going to make camp here for the night," he said.

The soldiers tended to the animals while Moses Calhoun made a shelter, picketing them nearby. The Indian boys without names collected firewood, dead branches lying on the ground. Aka Ne'ai sat with the injured soldier.

The shelters he had made for just himself had been small, easily constructed temporary shelters. Now, though, he felt he needed to build something the size of a cabin to accommodate all the refugees he was protecting.

He cut numerous spruce branches and a couple of long pine branches. He made a lean-to shelter using the long pine branches, and stacked the spruce branches from the ground up to make the walls of the shelter. He also cut spruce branches to lay down as a floor to keep the inhabitants off the wet ground.

He dug out a place for a fire near the shelter and used some spruce boughs to construct a wall that would funnel the heat from the fire into the shelter.

They used the blankets from the horse and ponies to make a floor, and they laid Chris Dolan down in the shelter near the fire.

Calhoun found pine needles that he boiled into a tea.

If the boy was taking infection or fever, the tea would help. He also boiled some venison with his last potato and onion to make a thick broth for Chris Dolan to drink, hoping it would be sustenance enough to build up his strength.

As he boiled the broth and tea, Calhoun talked to Craig Dolan.

"There is not much more I can do for your brother," Calhoun said. "The tea might keep him from taking a fever. The broth might help give him some strength back. Beyond that, it's on him to heal. We'll keep the fire fed through the night and try to keep him warm."

"Be tough to keep him warm," Hep Chandler said. "I'm about half froze, and nobody cut my shirt off of me."

Calhoun narrowed his eyes at the soldier.

"Next time you find yourself in these mountains on the cusp of winter, I'd advise you not to take your coat off," Calhoun said. "This is not a place to be caught without your coat."

Because it was his last onion and potato, Calhoun gave a share of the stew he'd boiled to the two soldiers, Aka Ne'ai and her children. He ate some for himself, but it did little to back down the pangs of hunger he felt.

He was poorly provisioned to get all these people off the mountain, and he wasn't taking enough food himself for all the energy he was expending.

"Coming around the back side of this mountain the way we are, we've added a couple of days to our journey," Calhoun said. "But if we get separated for some reason, you have to keep following around to the east side of the mountain, and then you have to find a trail that will drop you down to the valley below. You're still a hundred miles from town, but I reckon you'll cross with the rest of your soldiers down in the valley."

"What would separate us?" Craig Dolan said, feeling a moment of panic. He'd become convinced that his brother would die if it wasn't for this mountain hunter.

"Anything," Calhoun said. "Them Snake warriors, those two army scouts. I could trip and fall into the creek. Anything can happen, and you need to be prepared for it if it does."

"What about the Injun woman and the children?" Craig asked.

"I'd ask you to see to it that they get back to the town. Her father lives there, and I promised him that I would get her back to him."

Craig and Hep Chandler exchanged a glance.

"We'd do that, for sure," Hep Chandler said. "You've been good to help us when you didn't have to."

Moses Calhoun sniffed.

"We're not out of this yet," he said.

Craig and Hep were able to get the tea and the broth into Chris Dolan. He woke long enough to drink some of both. Then he slept for a while, but Craig woke him up and made him drink more of the broth. It was warm, and the taste of it was rich, and Chris Dolan took it eagerly. He didn't care as much for the pine tea, but he drank a cup of that, also. Chris managed to keep down both the broth and the tea, and Moses Calhoun watched for that. It was a sign that the boy might be able to mend. He smelled the boy's bandages and couldn't detect a scent that would suggest gangrene.

Calhoun kept the kettle with the pine tea near the

fire to keep it hot. There wasn't anything left of the broth. The others had eaten it all as a stew.

It was still not dark when everyone had eaten. They'd lost a lot of traveling time by stopping so early to make camp, but Calhoun was satisfied with his decision.

"I have to sleep," Calhoun said. "You boys stay awake and be alert. Watch that sorrel horse. If there's danger nearby, he'll alert to it. Give me a couple of hours, and then wake me up. I'll stand watch through the night and let the two of you sleep after that."

The mountain hunter wrapped himself in his bearskin coat and laid down at the edge of the shelter he built. He was asleep within moments.

- 22 -

The sorrel horse was standing on its picket, asleep.

Moses Calhoun had just put another small log on the fire. All the firewood the boys could gather was pine and spruce, and it made for a poor fire. Through the night, the fire crackled and spit sparks. The wood was all wet from the snow, but Calhoun had gotten a hot fire going in his pit, and each fresh log he put down dried out and burned quickly. He was already worried that he would run out of firewood before he ran out of the night's darkness.

Suddenly the horse picked up its head, his ears

pointed and turned forward. He was looking back the way they'd come.

The snow and fog, and the dark of night, made everything so black that Calhoun doubted any men would find their camp, even if they smelled the smoke. He'd buried the fire in a pit again, and he doubted anyone would see the light from the fire.

But the horse was unquestionably spooked by something.

Calhoun had one of the Colt Navy revolvers in his lap, and he slid his gloved-fist around its grip and cocked back the hammer.

It could be another mountain lion, stalking an easy meal. It might even be a bear, though the heavy snow made it unlikely to see a bear for a while.

It could be nothing, too. That sorrel horse was good at spooking at every danger, but it often spooked when there was nothing to fear. Or at least nothing that Calhoun was ever able to find.

He slid out of shelter, trying not to disturb the others, but a voice asked, "Is there something wrong?"

It was Craig Dolan.

"Might be nothing," Calhoun whispered.

The embers of the fire still glowed orange, only a small flame flickered up from the latest branch he had put into the fire pit. Calhoun moved quickly away from the fire so that he wouldn't be lit.

There was almost nothing to see in the dark woods. Whatever moonlight might be overhead cast no light through the heavy cloud cover. Flakes of snow still drifted lazily through the woods, but Calhoun wasn't sure if these were loose flakes blown by the breeze down from the branches or if it was still snowing. There would be a foot or more now in the open places if it was still snowing.

He stepped lightly, hoping to avoid making any sound, and when he was several steps away from the shelter and the light of the fire now, and he stood motionless, listening to the sounds of the forest.

Snow broke free from a branch somewhere and fell with a crash through the branches and hit the ground.

The light breeze whistled in the tree tops.

Something crunched in a patch of snow, and not far away.

Calhoun had his hand on the head of his hatchet, and he now slid it from its leather strap on his belt.

It might be an animal, but it might also be a person, attracted by the scent of the fire.

He heard another crunch of snow, and then another.

Calhoun knew that cougars seldom traveled together, unless it was a small family. Wolves hunted in packs, but they were seldom silent hunters. If wolves were nearby, Calhoun was confident he would have known they were close.

And then the crunching came rapidly, chaotic, thrashing through the branches of the spruce trees.

Whatever he'd heard was charging the shelter.

Calhoun crouched low, tightening his grip on the hatchet.

And there, in the dim, orange light of the fire, he saw what he'd heard. Two men rushing at the shelter.

Calhoun had a clear run.

He rushed forward and leapt, crashing heavily into one of the men, and bringing his hatchet down at the man's skull.

He was sure it was the two army scouts, but then from not far away he heard a loud, high-pitched and undulating yell, and realized the Snake warriors had tracked them through the night and were mounting their attack.

The man below him went limp with the blow to the head. Calhoun heard the crack of bone and saw the dark liquid spreading over his face.

At the mouth of the shelter, Calhoun heard a shot. Craig Dolan came out of the shelter with one of the Colt Navy revolvers in his hand. He'd shot the Indian closest to the shelter. Hep Chandler stepped out beside him. He also had one of the revolvers.

The melee in the black night was confused and chaotic.

Calhoun fought the way he would fight against a mountain lion. He swung the hatchet at everything. He pulled his Bowie knife in his left hand and held it downward in a fighting style so that he could punch with the grip and cut either by slicing up or down.

He swung left and right with the hatchet, sometimes feeling it make contact with enemies he could not see, and some of the swings went wild and missed everything.

Calhoun felt hands gripping at him. A knife or spear caught him in the side. He lunged with the hatchet and felt it bury deep in a shoulder

The two soldiers also fought. Anything that

211

approached the shelter they shot at as long as they had bullets. In the orange light of the fire, Moses Calhoun saw the flash from a gun and a warrior slung back as if jerked from behind.

There was shouting in the Snake language, and Calhoun could hear Aka Ne'ai in the shelter shouting back at the warriors.

Someone grabbed Moses Calhoun by the shoulder and spun him, and he knew by the way the man grabbed him that he intended to stab Calhoun. He threw up an arm to try to deflect the weapon coming at him, and he felt the blade slice through the heavy bearskin coat.

He swung hard with the hatchet and heard a sharp gasp as the heavy, ball end cracked against flesh and bone, and then his shoulder was free.

Calhoun heard rushing through the trees, but the sound was diminishing. The Indian warriors had given up the fight.

And then the stillness of the dark night returned.

Calhoun stumbled back toward the shelter, exhausted from the fight.

He collapsed near the opening of the shelter, near enough to feel the heat of the fire. He was breathing hard, and with each intake of breath, he could feel the smoke from the fire in his throat.

"Reload your guns," Calhoun said. "They'll be back."

The two soldiers ducked back down into the shelter. Hep Chandler threw a couple of dry branches onto the fire to kick up the flames so that they had light to see to reload their guns.

"You're hurt," Craig Dolan said.

"Not bad," Calhoun said.

The two soldiers reloaded their guns, and then they pulled Calhoun into the shelter. It was exhaustion more than his injuries, but Calhoun felt himself drifting off.

He was aware of Aka Ne'ai and one of the soldiers taking his heavy jacket off of him. He sat up for them to pull his buckskin shirt over his head. He was vaguely aware of Aka Ne'ai tending to his injuries.

And the next thing he knew, the light of dawn shone outside the shelter.

Craig Dolan was already out of the shelter walking around.

"We killed one," he said. "One body out here, anyway. But there's blood all over."

In his sleep, Aka Ne'ai had tucked Calhoun's bearskin coat around him. He sat up now, and felt the freezing cold against his bare chest and back. His buckskin shirt had two holes in, and his own blood had stained the shirt at the holes.

He looked down at his arm. The cut was not deep. Aka Ne'ai had put some of his salve on it. The heavy coat had kept the blade from cutting deep, and the wound on his arm was little more than a scratch.

But the wound in his side was worse. It was a stab wound and had bled through the bandage Aka Ne'ai had put on it.

He took the bandage off and stretched to look at himself. Stretching caused a sharp pain. The bleeding had stopped while he slept. Aka Ne'ai had used the salve on the wound and bandaged it tightly. It was tender and hurt, but once again, Calhoun believed his heavy bearskin coat and the thick buckskin shirt prevented the wound from being as serious as it might have been.

"I'll wrap it," Aka Ne'ai said, watching him. She took a fresh bandage and wrapped his ribs again. That left them with only two bandages left.

When she was finished, Calhoun dressed himself and started folding blankets to put them back in the pannier.

"We need to move quickly," he told the others. "Those Snake warriors will likely be back, and I don't want to be here waiting for them."

"You won't object if we hold onto our revolvers?" Craig Dolan said.

"I reckon not," Calhoun said.

As they packed their gear, Aka Ne'ai spoke to Calhoun.

"The warriors will not come back," she said. "I could hear them shouting to each other during the fight. They were badly hurt, many of them."

Calhoun remained impassive.

"Maybe," he said.

But as he surveyed the area where the fighting took place, he saw that Craig Dolan had not overstated the scene of the battle.

In the place where Moses Calhoun had fought, the snow was dark with blood. Some of it was his own, but he had been more effective with the hatchet and the knife than he even realized. And there was a dead man on the ground, his skull split open like a watermelon.

Near the shelter, there were several places where the evidence suggested the two soldiers had been effective with their revolvers, splatters of blood in the snow. Calhoun found trails of blood leading deeper into the woods. The warriors had taken a beating. The soldiers must have shot four or five of them, and Moses himself had delivered serious wounds to a couple of them, in addition to the one he'd killed.

Perhaps Aka Ne'ai was correct.

***

Calhoun's prediction that the warriors were not finished with them proved true sooner than he expected.

The small party had just started to move when the attack came.

Moses Calhoun had decided to get down to the ledge overlooking the canyon cut by the river. They had camped nearby, and he knew it was solid stone here without trees or undergrowth to impede them. Even in the snow they were able to move faster than they could through the ferns and spruce branches blocking their way in the forest. He did not like the thought of being backed against the steep drop into the gorge, but he felt his group had to get away as fast as possible.

As they'd done the day before, Moses Calhoun walked his horse and mule. The two children doubled up on one pony. Aka Ne'ai rode another pony, and the wounded soldier sat on the third pony. The other two soldiers walked alongside to keep an eye on Chris Dolan, but the young boy was healthier than he'd been the day before. He was hurting, but he was conscious now, and though he was still weak, he was mostly able to hold himself upright on the pony.

The fog hung thick in the gorge so that they could not even see the falls and the rushing rapids of the river, but it was thinner along the ledge and the snow had stopped. The clouds above seemed to be burning off, and Calhoun expected they would see the sun – it would prove to be a grateful sight.

They'd gone only a mile along the edge of the canyon when Moses Calhoun heard in the woods the rush of the attack.

He snatched his hatchet from his belt and turned to face them.

A warrior leapt clear from the trees and emerged on the trail not fifteen feet from where Calhoun stood. The man let loose a frightful war cry.

He held in his grip a long spear, decorated with feathers and beads. He raised the spear over his head.

Moses Calhoun charged forward.

He knew in close combat the best defense was to get inside the attack as fast as possible. If Calhoun could get face to face with the man, it would render that spear all but useless.

The warrior swung down with the spear just as Moses Calhoun slammed into him, and the two men went down in a tumbling heap, back toward the trees.

Both of the soldiers fired their guns behind him, trying to drive back enemies that Calhoun had not seen.

Moses Calhoun and the warrior grappled close, each trying to gain a position on the other. Calhoun held the man's wrist away and absorbed first one punch and then another. Both hits were upper-cuts to the side of his head, but Calhoun held the man in a tight embrace, preventing the warrior from getting leverage on him.

Now Moses Calhoun struck. He rolled the grip of the hatchet in his hand so that it was facing back toward him, and then he swung the blade down into the shoulder of the warrior. The sharp edge of the hatchet tore through the warrior's tunic, and as Calhoun dragged it down, he could feel the hatchet tearing into flesh and muscle.

The warrior howled and jerked himself away. The man was staggered by the pain, and the hatchet had torn so deeply into his back and shoulder that he could not lift his arm. He'd dropped the spear. He faced Calhoun for a breath, and then he turned, scrambling back into the woods.

Calhoun turned to find the soldiers standing on guard, their revolvers up, searching for a target.

Craig Dolan stood over a fallen Snake warrior. Calhoun backed up, near to the soldiers. The warrior at Dolan's feet appeared to be dead, and Calhoun saw that he was bleeding from three bullet wounds in his chest.

"How many more did you see?" Calhoun asked.

"I shot one other in the woods," Hep Chandler said.

"I saw two more, maybe three," Craig Dolan said. "They both turned and ran when I shot this one."

"That's it," Moses Calhoun said. "If the best they could muster was five or six warriors to come after us, there won't be another attack. That was their last effort. Just trying to save face against the failed attack last night."

"You think so?" Craig Dolan asked.

Calhoun nodded.

He glanced back at Aka Ne'ai. She was looking in

horror at the man lying dead at Craig Dolan's feet.

"Are you hurt?" Calhoun asked her, surprised by the look on her face.

She shook her head silently. Then said, "I am not hurt. I know that man."

Calhoun nodded.

"They shouldn't have come after us," he said.

"They thought you led the soldiers to us," Aka Ne'ai said, still looking at the dead man.

"They should have listened to Chief Mukuakantun who told them I did not."

Aka Ne'ai nodded sadly.

"Yes, they should have," she said.

Somewhere above them, higher up the slope, a man began to shout in the Snake language. Aka Ne'ai turned her head, listening to him.

"My name is Three Black Feathers," Aka Ne'ai translated. "I will come for you Lion Killer."

Calhoun took a deep breath and then he shouted back.

"I am Tekaiten Toi-yah-'to'ko!" he yelled. "I fear no man. If you come for me, I will kill you."

The man in the woods continued to shout, even after Moses Calhoun took up the lead rope on the sorrel horse and started his party moving again. Repeating the same threat over and over again. "My name is Three Black Feathers. I will come for you Lion Killer!"

Exhausted from the fight and his injuries sustained during the night, Moses Calhoun walked on for some distance before finally deciding to mount the horse and ride. The pain in his side burned like fire as he stretched his leg to swing it over the sorrel's saddle. He felt moisture on his side and knew that he'd reopened the wound and that it was bleeding again. He pressed his elbow against the wound, hoping to give it enough pressure that it would close back and stop bleeding.

- 23 -

Chester Klemp had meat stored up for the winter, but he didn't want to get into it until he had to. When the sun came up, he decided to get out an enjoy the sunshine and see if he couldn't scare up a rabbit or two. The truth was, the best time to shoot rabbit was in the evening, but sometimes he could get lucky and find one just after sunup.

He'd gone a couple of miles from his cabin, sticking to the paths he typically took on his morning hunts. There were plenty of mountain hunters and trappers around who knew their way and could wander hither and thither in search of game, but Chester Klemp was not one of those. He was getting better at surviving on his own, and did not fear the winter the way he once did. But he did fear getting too far from home and getting lost.

He smelled the smoke and should have suspected it meant trouble, but his first thought was of Moses Calhoun. So he wandered toward the smoke, keeping his eyes open for rabbits along the way.

In a small clearing he saw a fire, three horses tied nearby. Huddled together, without shelter or blanket and nothing more than heavy woolen coats and a fire of soft pine wood to keep them warm.

"You boys look about half froze," Chester Klemp said, walking toward them.

Two of three the three men lifted heavy Colt revolvers and pointed them at Klemp, but he raised up his hands, holding his rifle high over his head so they could see he wasn't going to shoot at them.

"Whoa, now," Klemp said. "I don't mean you no harm."

"Where the hell did you come from?" Sergeant Terry demanded.

"I've got a place back yonder a ways," Chester Klemp said. "I guess the surprise isn't finding me here, but finding you here."

Chester Klemp had no love for the army, but he couldn't leave these men to freeze to death. As he looked at one of them, the boy had a faraway stare and he was pale. Chester squinted at him, looking for wounds.

"Is he all right?" Chester asked. "He looks like he's seen ghost."

The older of the three men, the one with the sergeant's stripes, glanced at the soldier.

"He's seen something," the sergeant said.

"Is he hurt?" Chester said.

"He ain't hurt," the sergeant answered, but the boy seemed oblivious of the conversation about him.

"Come on, then," he said. "You can come back to my cabin, get warm and dry yourselves out. I've got a pot of stew on the fire."

Sergeant Terry looked at the two others. They had all made it through the pass and survived the night, and this man had shown up like an angel from Heaven. The men couldn't feel their toes, and it took some doing for Chester to help them up off the ground and get them moving. But in time, they worked their way down to the path that was marked enough that Chester could find it to get home.

The men did not talk as they walked, other than to occasionally ask how much farther it was to the cabin.

When they arrived at the cabin, Chester ushered the men inside and put a couple of extra logs on the fire. He dished up stew for the three soldiers. Then he went outside to deal with their horses, leaving their saddles under the overhang on the front porch. The horses went straight to the hay that he'd put out, and Chester Klemp frowned thinking about the small supply he had for his own animals.

Inside, Chester pressed the men to find out what they were doing and why they were so high up in the mountains. His concern was that they were looking for him, though he couldn't believe the army would be coming after him on the warrants he'd accumulated down below. All the same, when he introduced himself to the soldiers, he told them his name was Raymond.

"We've come up with a patrol of twenty-four men,"

Sergeant Terry said. "Two scouts, too. We were looking for Injuns."

Chester Klemp nodded. He understood now. This was the scouting party for the soldiers Moses Calhoun had told him about.

"Well, if there was twenty-six of you to start, and not but three now, I'd say you found them."

"We found them," one of the soldiers said.

"We're just trying to find our way back to our regiment," Sergeant Terry said.

"Where is the regiment?" Chester asked.

"They should be approaching the pass in a day or two," Sergeant Terry said. "We're not sure exactly where they are. But they'll be coming the same way we came."

Chester nodded thoughtfully. He doubted the patrol had come this way and not stopped at his cabin, particularly if they had experienced scouts with them. That probably meant they approached the pass from farther north, which would make sense if they were coming from town.

"Well, you're too far to the south, I'd reckon. I imagine your regiment will be coming into the pass from the north," Chester said.

Sergeant Terry pursed his lips, but he was beyond caring.

"There any wounded back behind you?" Chester asked.

"We don't know," Terry said. "Them Injun bastards hit our camp at dawn. The three of us got away, maybe some others. But they killed our lieutenant. Last I saw, they were butchering every one of our men they could lay hands on."

Chester dished himself up some stew. He'd not eaten any breakfast in his desire to get out and look for rabbits, and now he was feeling a knot in his stomach.

"I expect them Injuns will get paid back in kind soon enough," Chester said.

"Can you help us get to our regiment?" Sergeant Terry asked, ignoring the comment.

"Maybe," Chester said.

One of the other soldiers, the one who looked injured though he had no visible wounds, suddenly spoke up.

"It was that damn mountain man," he said. "He led them Injuns right to us."

"I don't think he did, son," Sergeant Terry said.

"Then how did they find us, and come on us the way they did?" the soldier asked. "They come on us so fast, and it was terrible what they done. They hacked all our men. Did you see how they came at the lieutenant? They chopped him up like a beef cow. They chopped them all like beeves."

"What mountain man is that?" Chester asked, interrupting. They boy seemed to be speaking out of his head, anyway.

Sergeant Terry narrowed his eyes, studying Chester Klemp.

"Man named Moses Calhoun," Terry said. "We had him for a while as our prisoner, but he escaped from us. You know the man?"

Chester nodded slightly.

"I know him," Chester said. "I doubt he'd lead Indians after you, though."

"He didn't," Sergeant Terry said. "We were chasing behind him. But he probably warned the Indians we were coming. Either way, I expect the army will hang that man if Bearclaw Jim don't get him first."

"Who is Bearclaw Jim?" Chester asked.

"Our scout. That friend of yourn shot Bearclaw Jim's finger and thumb clean off," Sergeant Terry explained. "I expect Bearclaw Jim will be looking for Moses Calhoun until he finds him."

Chester gave up the conversation. Talking to the soldiers quickly reminded him how much he didn't miss being down below.

The men sat around Chester's fire, their boots and socks off and their feet pushed as close to the fire as they could tolerate. Chester looked for signs of frostbite, but the men had made it through the night without suffering any permanent damage. If it had been another month or so later into the winter, these soldiers would not fared so well.

The soldiers were hopelessly lost and all turned around. They'd taken mountain trails without the aid of the sun to tell them which way they were going. He questioned them about the landmarks they saw when they'd first come to the pass from the town, and from their answers Chester was able to figure out which way their regiment would be coming up.

"I'll take you out where you'll find your regiment, Sergeant," Chester Klemp said. "I can give you provisions enough to last you a couple of days."

"We'd be obliged to you," Sergeant Terry said.

Sergeant Terry couldn't ask anything more of Chester Klemp, though he would have liked to leave the raving man behind.

"We'll set out in the morning," Klemp said. "We can get up to the pass, and I'll leave you where your regiment will come through. If you don't see them in a day or two, you can make your way back here and I'll figure out how to get you to the town."

Even with provisions, Chester Klemp didn't know if the men would survive long enough to reunite with their regiment. But he did not care. He wanted them out of his cabin.

So in the morning he took them back to the pass. He found them a place where they could put up a shelter and get a good fire going and have a view of the pass. If the regiment came through there, they'd see it. By early afternoon, Chester Klemp was on his way back to his cabin.

For the next few days, Chester half expected that the soldiers would turn up at his cabin, but they never did. He saw nothing more of the soldiers, leaving him to assume they must have successfully rejoined their regiment. Months later, in the late spring, Chester Klemp even made the half-day journey up to the pass, to the place where he had last seen them, and looked to see if their bodies were there.

Finding no evidence of them, Chester then wondered how many people the soldiers he saved killed at the Snake People's winter camp.

- 24 -

Following the creek upstream, the rapids below rose higher, the canyon grew less deep. Calhoun knew that following the ledge over the canyon was taking them to the east side of the mountain, and from there they could drop down in the valley and the journey home would be much easier. They would be on open ground, and maybe if the day of sunshine turned into two or three days of sunshine, it would melt the snow sufficient to give them easy going.

Most of the fog had burned off now, and the sun's ray warmed the travelers out on the exposed ledge.

Moses Calhoun shed the bearskin coat that had helped to protect him in the overnight attack, but the wind whipped into the fresh holes in his buckskin shirt and felt cool against the wounds. The stab wound in his side had stopped bleeding, but he knew the wound was a mess. The sooner he got home, the better chance he would have to better deal with the wound. They had only a tiny amount of salve left, and Calhoun had decided to save that for young Chris Dolan.

Around midday, Calhoun realized that they were no longer hiking up. They topped the ridge that marked the line from the east side to the west side of the mountain. He knew, too, that they would need to cut away from the stream. The creek had its beginnings farther to the south, climbing higher up into the mountains where a series of clear mountain lakes produced the streams that came together to form the creek.

"Keep walking along the canyon here," Moses told the two soldiers. "I'm going to ride ahead and see if I can find a good place for us to cut down into the valley."

Calhoun took a look at Chris Dolan. The exertion of riding was making him weak again, and Calhoun feared he had a fever coming on. The boy needed a bed and warmth and food.

He mounted the sorrel horse and urged it forward, along the rim of the canyon. Soon the others were out of sight.

The creek was twisting away from the eastern valley where Calhoun wanted to be, and he soon found himself climbing again, higher into the mountains. But after a couple of miles, he came to a wide meadow that sloped down toward the east. A blanket of snow covered the meadow, and spruce trees grew scattered out across it.

And Calhoun could see that the meadow slowly rolled down toward the valley below.

The view gave Calhoun his first sight of the eastern valley that would take him home, and he felt stronger just seeing it.

Always in the back of his mind he thought of the warmth of his cabin, his two sons, and his wife, and now visions of warm meals and a warm fireplace occupied his imagination, and he wished that he had some power to pinch the land and step from one mountain to the next without having to cross the long valley.

The valley appeared to be covered in a thick blanket of snow. They might find the forest trails where the snow did not pile quite as thick to be easier going when they reached the base of the mountain, but in places they would have no choice but to go through the open meadows of the valley.

Satisfied that he'd found what he was looking for, Calhoun wheeled the horse and rode back to the others who were still making their slow trek along the rim of the canyon.

"Did you find the right trail?" Craig Dolan asked.

"I think I did," Calhoun told him. "It's still a long way ahead of us to get your brother to a place of safety, but we're getting closer."

"How long?" Hep Chandler asked. "It's been a long time since I've felt my toes."

Calhoun frowned.

"Four days through the valley if we push hard," Calhoun said. "The snow will make it rough going and slower than I'd like."

Craig Dolan looked at his younger brother. Chris had started the day so well, awake and with strength enough to sit straight in the saddle. But now he was slumped, and he seemed to be out of his head, though his eyes were open.

"Does he have four days?" Craig asked.

"He'll have to," Moses Calhoun said. "He has no choice."

Chris Dolan was not the only one that Calhoun worried about.

Aka Ne'ai and the children seemed sluggish through the morning. It might simply be lack of sleep after the nighttime attack, but Calhoun knew no one was getting sufficient nourishment.

So he pushed the little group to move faster.

They cut out through the open meadow and Moses Calhoun found a wooded draw on the down side that gave them a nice slope to get down off the mountain.

They camped that night in the draw, Calhoun opting for two smaller shelters instead of one large one. He showed the soldiers how to make the first shelter, talking them through how to weave the spruce boughs to provide both a tight break from the cold and a, mostly, rain-proof shelter. And then he watched while the soldiers made the second shelter.

He saw a doe picking its way through the draw down below them, but he decided not to risk a shot. There were too many people on this mountain to be announcing his presence in such a fashion.

"I've hunted these mountains for the better part of the last ten years," Moses Calhoun told the soldiers while they worked on the second shelter. "I've been up here where you could walk for days and never see another living soul. Now, it's so crowded up here that you can't move on this mountain without bumping into someone."

"It's about to get worse," Craig Dolan said. "If the regiment isn't already up here, it will be soon."

Calhoun nodded.

"They're going to make light work of those Indians back at that camp," Calhoun said. "You boys should be glad you're not there."

"I'd be happy to pay them back for what they done to our patrol," Hep Chandler said. "Billy Douglas. The lieutenant. All them others, just butchered."

Calhoun nodded to the entrance of the first shelter where Aka Ne'ai's sons watched the soldiers weaving spruce boughs.

"If you was to ride in with your regiment and attack that camp, you wouldn't be fighting many warriors. Boys like them two there would be your enemies," Calhoun said. "You'd live a long time with the memory of shooting a boy like that, or cutting him down with your saber."

Hep Chandler looked at Aka Ne'ai's sons and nodded vaguely.

"Maybe so," he said.

"I ain't never going back to the army," Craig Dolan said. "When we get out of here, I'll be buying some regular clothes and burying this uniform, and I'm making my way back to California."

Hep pushed a limb from one branch under the limb of another branch.

"Yep, I reckon I'll go with you."

Moses Calhoun nodded.

"Nothing wrong with being an independent man and picking your own fights," he said.

That night, Calhoun had enough meat to make only the thinnest of broths for Chris Dolan. There wasn't meat enough to go around, and Calhoun had to be satisfied with just a half of the last biscuit. He had a little bit of flour, but he decided to save that, and when he sat up on watch that night, his backbone was snatching at his belt buckle so bad that he regretted not risking the shot on the doe.

In the morning he would have to hunt.

***

Moses Calhoun sent the others ahead, telling them to follow the draw.

"Likely it'll hit a switchback or level out," he told Craig Dolan. "If you get to a place that is impassible, then just hold there and wait for me. Otherwise, you keep following the natural terrain down toward the valley. I'll be along as quick as I can."

Calhoun thought well of Craig Dolan, and he knew that the older brother felt the responsibility of getting his younger brother to safety. For that reason, Calhoun treated Dolan as his lieutenant – when he needed something done, he put it on Craig Dolan's shoulders to do it.

"If you make the valley before I return, find a spot under the trees to camp," Calhoun told him. "Make a couple of small shelters. Dig a fire pit. I'll be along."

"What if something happens to you?" Craig Dolan asked. "What if you don't show up?"

Moses Calhoun pursed his lips and considered it.

"Doubtful as it is, if I don't show up, you make your way east across this valley. It's a long haul and will take you a couple of days, maybe three. But you just keep going east. Eventually you'll hit a small settlement, just a few dozen houses and a trading post. They can get you to the town. And you tell them to send word to my wife that I won't be coming back."

He gave them the mule to take, but Calhoun kept the sorrel horse with him. He wouldn't be able to ride the horse to catch up to them, not unless they made the valley, and that was doubtful. But he would want the horse to take the carcass if he shot a deer or an elk.

He left the others and climbed a ways higher up the mountain, looking for a clearing where he might have a better chance at seeing a deer. He had his rifle loaded and primed, ready to go the moment he saw something, so he stepped carefully.

The horse followed along behind him, never more than ten or twenty yards away, but Calhoun didn't drag the lead rope. The sorrel was good about following without being told to.

An hour had gone by, maybe more. Calhoun was not terribly far from where they had camped the night before, though he guessed that the rest of his party was making its way lower and was now well away from him. He'd catch them, he knew, but he might not see them much before nightfall if he didn't quick find something to shoot.

He came to a place where the trees thinned, not a

clearing exactly, but enough space between the spruce trees that he could see for some distance. Here he decided to stop for a while and wait to see what came along.

He'd left at first light, and it was still early enough in the morning that the deer should be active.

He stood waiting. The sorrel horse had come over near him, and he rubbed the horse's neck.

He heard a noise but didn't rush to find the source. A light step in the snow somewhere not far in front of him. He didn't see anything right away, but he knew if he waited, he'd have an opportunity. And then a couple more steps. Calhoun moved out from behind the sorrel horse and dropped down to one knee, raising his rifle up to his shoulder. A couple more steps in the snow, and then, about thirty yards away, a doe stepped out into the clear. Its head was down, rooting in the snow for grass to eat.

He let out his breath, aiming small.

The doe lifted its head to sniff the air. Calhoun's aim followed the raised head. On the exhale, he squeezed the trigger. The flint dropped, the pan sparked, the powder ignited. With an almighty crack that made the sorrel jump, the Poor-Boy rifle bought Moses Calhoun and his small party dinner for the next few nights.

He field dressed the doe there where it fell and then tied the carcass to a stout pine branch to let it cool with sticks holding it open. It wouldn't take long to let the deer cool in this weather. While the deer cooled, Calhoun found a pile of snow that he used to clean his hands of the doe's blood.

Though he was idle now, waiting for the deer to be

ready to move, he stayed alert.

Mostly all he heard was his own stomach gnawing at him. Over the past few days he'd spent so much energy, and he'd not taken on enough food to keep himself going. Just thinking of the meal he would have later made him feel a bit light-headed.

The sorrel was grazing down below him at the edge of the thicker woods where the snow didn't quite blanket all the undergrowth.

And from up above, Calhoun heard movement. It sounded distinctly human to the hunter's ears.

He'd reloaded the Colt six-shooter, thinking he might use that if he happened upon a rabbit, and now he grabbed tight to the gun and spun around. He did not immediately see whatever it was he'd heard, but that didn't mean what he'd heard didn't see him. Calhoun quickly side-stepped away from where he was in case someone was drawing a bead on him. He ducked down behind the branches of a spruce tree, and that's where he was when he heard the voices, very near and very clear.

"I tell you, that shot came from around here," Bearclaw Jim said. "I reckon I can pinpoint a rifle shot."

Moses Calhoun touched a spruce branch in front of him to press it down just a touch so that he could see. There they were, Bearclaw Jim and Jack Cut Face. Jim's hand was wrapped in a bandage. The Lakota Scout carried a Lancaster rifle across his folded arms, and Calhoun noted the flintlock was on half-cock.

"Look there," the Lakota scout said, pointing to where Calhoun had dressed the deer. There was blood and organs from the doe in the snow.

With his good hand, Bearclaw Jim drew his Bowie

knife.

"He's here somewhere," he said, glancing around.

Just then, the sorrel raised up its head and snorted.

Both men started at the noise. Bearclaw Jim took a step back behind Jack Cut Face. The Lakota scout raised up his rifle. The two men side-stepped around a spruce tree and the sorrel came into view for them. Now they were speaking to each other in whispers that Moses Calhoun could not hear. He was certain they had not seen him, but they knew he was nearby.

Moses Calhoun winced as he drew back the hammer on the Colt Navy. As it clicked at full cock, both the Lakota scout and Bearclaw Jim looked directly at him.

Jack Cut Face leveled the rifle and fired without taking aim.

The .48-caliber ball split through the branches of the spruce tree. Moses Calhoun dove away from the tree and landed on his back. He rolled quickly and pulled the trigger on the Colt Navy. But he was too late to shoot. He fired into the spruce tree, aiming at the place where he'd last seen the two men, but they had scrambled away after Jack Cut Face fired his shot.

Calhoun tried to fire again, but the percussion cap was a dud. There wasn't time to even try another shot. The two men were coming at him.

The Lakota scout tossed away his rifle and drew a long Arkansas Toothpick fighting knife. He was coming around the tree at Calhoun's right.

Bearclaw Jim, his Bowie knife in his one good hand, came around at Calhoun's left.

Calhoun scrambled to his feet, both hands reaching

to his belt.

His right fist came out with his hatchet, and his left gripped his Bowie knife.

As the two men advanced on him, Moses Calhoun swung a wide arc with the hatchet to keep them back. He followed with a couple more wide swings, holding the hatchet low on the handle and keeping his Bowie knife ready near his body.

When he swung a third time with the hatchet, Jack Cut Face stepped into the space and tried a jab with his knife. Calhoun jumped away and the slung the hatchet back quickly. They heavy ball-head of the hatchet cracked hard against the Lakota's shoulder.

As Calhoun swung back with the hatchet at the Lakota, Bearclaw Jim stepped in to try a swipe with his knife. Calhoun sliced the air with his own knife, trying to slash Bearclaw Jim, but the man jumped back quickly to avoid the knife.

The man moved with fear. Half his hand shot away, he was like a kicked dog that didn't want to get kicked again.

The realization came to Calhoun in a second, but he knew immediately that Bearclaw Jim presented the lesser of the two threats.

He charged at Jack Cut Face, slashing with his knife.

The two men came together and toppled to the ground. They rolled, and Jack Cut Face got over Moses Calhoun, straddling him. He raised up his knife, ready to bring it down and impale Calhoun.

"Kill him!" Bearclaw Jim encouraged the Lakota scout.

Moses Calhoun brought his knee up, crashing it hard into Jack Cut Face's tailbone. The blow threw the man off balance, and Calhoun pushed the man off him. Calhoun rolled and pushed himself up to his feet.

He was breathing heavy, and his side was wet with blood again where the stab wound had again reopened.

Jack Cut Face sprang to his feet, too, and the Lakota scout started to charge.

Calhoun swung the hatchet high over his head and then slung it down, throwing it at the Lakota scout who stood just a few feet away. The hatchet turned one time over before the blade hit Jack Cut Face in the gut, and there it stayed.

The Lakota stumbled, and Moses Calhoun was on him in a heartbeat.

Calhoun wrenched the hatchet from the man's gut, exposing a vicious wound. As he moved, Calhoun rolled the Bowie knife in his hand so that the blade was pointing forward. He rammed it hard into the man's chest.

Jack Cut Face stumbled backwards half a step. All the fight was slipping out of him as Calhoun pulled back the knife. Once more, Moses Calhoun swung the hatchet, catching Jack Cut Face in the side of the skull with the ball-head. Calhoun could hear the bone crack.

The Lakota's eyes glazed over and he fell to the ground.

Now Calhoun turned toward Bearclaw Jim. He was standing ten yards away, watching in surprise as his partner dropped away from the fight.

The white scout had found Calhoun's Navy revolver

and was holding it out in front of him.

"I'm sorry to see you kill him," Bearclaw Jim said. "He was a right good traveling partner for a long time. But I reckon he'll be satisfied knowing you're coming right behind him."

Calhoun gripped the hatchet, ready to make a run at Bearclaw Jim.

Jim thumbed back the hammer on the Colt Navy, and with a final grin he squeezed the trigger. The hammer fell on another dud percussion cap.

Calhoun sprang forward, but Bearclaw Jim flung the gun at him.

Calhoun parried it away with the hatchet, and watched as Bearclaw Jim turned and started to run up the slope.

Moses Calhoun slid his Bowie knife down into its sheath on his belt and reached his hand to his bleeding side, squeezing it to try to give it enough pressure to stop bleeding.

He felt sick and faint, and as he took another step to follow Bearclaw Jim up the slope, Calhoun's legs wobbled and he stumbled to his knees.

He knelt there for a while, trying to get his strength back.

He did not like the idea of letting Bearclaw Jim get away, but he also did not want to pass out from blood loss while trying to catch Bearclaw Jim and then, potentially, be at the man's mercy.

When Moses Calhoun felt strong enough, he stood up from the ground and walked slowly back down to where he'd hung the doe carcass. He cut it down and struggled to get the doe onto his horse where he tied it securely.

He gathered up his rifle and the Colt Navy revolver with the useless percussion caps, and he started back down the slope with the sorrel following.

BLOOD ON THE MOUNTAIN

- 25 -

Leaving Bearclaw Jim alive felt like the wrong thing to do.

As wide and grand as the mountains were, this territory could also be a small place, as Moses Calhoun had realized in these recent days. It wasn't uncommon to walk into another man's campsite while on a long hunt. Folks had a way of appearing in unexpected places. And Moses had been in these mountains long enough that he knew most all the white folks who had cabins in the wilderness, and they knew him. It would not be hard, if he desired, for Bearclaw Jim to come and find him.

Of lesser concern to him was the Snake warrior Pahates A'ni Sia-pin, Three Black Feathers.

Like as not, every fighting man in that snake village would be dead in a few days.

But Moses Calhoun was a man who did not have enemies. He treated all men he encountered decently and as equals, and when he could not do that, he avoided the man. But in the space of just a few days, he had made enemies among the Snake People where he had always found friends and among the white soldiers.

He followed the draw through the afternoon. As he suspected, it hit a rock face and switched back to reach lower toward the valley.

Despite his weakness and the pain in his side from the wound that kept reopening, Calhoun walked with the sorrel horse behind him.

Late in the day, he found the slope leveling out into the valley. The draw turned into just a narrow dry wash, though come spring it would fill with the runoff of melting snow and feed some bigger stream cutting through the valley.

It did not take long, then, to find the rest of his small group. Calhoun was still among the spruce and pine when he smelled smoke in the air, and he followed that until he walked into a grove of aspen trees.

Craig Dolan had made a shelter among the aspens, right at the edge of the spruce trees where he was able to gather the boughs for the shelters. He and Hep Chandler were already weaving aspen branches together, and Aka Ne'ai was tending to a campfire. The two boys were running among the trees, ostensibly gathering firewood, but mostly just laughing and playing.

Dolan drew his Colt Navy when he heard Moses Calhoun and the sorrel walking through the snow and leaves, but when he saw who it was, he holstered the gun.

"Wasn't sure you would ever catch up to us," Craig Dolan said.

"Ran into a bit of trouble," Calhoun said. "Them two scouts with your patrol jumped me. The Lakota is dead, but Bearclaw Jim is still somewhere up on the mountain."

Dolan showed no emotion, turning back to his work.

"I never did like them scouts, anyway," Hep Chandler said.

Chris Dolan was near the fire, bundled in blankets, but he was awake and he had an alert look in his eyes for the first time since joining Calhoun's party. As Calhoun approached the fire, he saw that Aka Ne'ai had a pot on the fire, and he recognized right away that she was boiling in water the stringy, inner bark of the aspen. He saw on a tree nearby where she had shaved away the outer bark and cut slices from the inner bark.

"That tea is about the best thing to ease his pain and back down that fever," Moses said.

Aka Ne'ai nodded her head. She poured some of the tea into a cup and handed it to Moses.

"You drink some, too," she said.

Calhoun drank the tea she offered to him. It didn't have much taste to it, but he'd had tea made from aspen bark enough times that the familiarity of it made him feel a little better almost immediately. He was grateful for the warmth of it, too. When he'd finished the last of the tea in the cup, Calhoun cut the tenderloin from the deer and made a spit over the fire to roast it. He also cut some pieces of meat for Aka Ne'ai to boil to make a thick broth for Chris Dolan.

By the time he was done, the two soldiers had finished their shelters, and Calhoun crawled inside one and slept for a little while. When he woke, he ate some of the venison. Everyone's mood improved with a full belly.

Come morning, the group set out, and Chris Dolan was able to sit upright for hours with only a little pain. His strength was returning to him, and the fever seemed diminished if not entirely gone.

They cut out through the valley meadow. The sun gave them some warmth, and by midday, most of the snow was melted. The two soldiers and Calhoun took turns riding and walking, and they made decent time through the day.

Several times, Calhoun kept his rifle and some shot and powder back with him and watched the back trail, allowing the others to keep moving.

He never saw any sign of someone following.

They traveled through the valley for the better part of three days. The weather held good for them, warm sun in the afternoons and no more snow, and late on the third day they reached the trail that would take them up to Calhoun's cabin on the mountain to their north.

"We'll camp here for the night," Calhoun told Craig Dolan. "In the morning, we'll go our separate ways. I'll take Aka Ne'ai and her children with me to my home. The three of you can follow this valley to the settlement at the end. You're half a day away. From there, folks can get you back to town."

In the morning, the party split up.

"I guess we're obliged to you, Mister Calhoun," Craig Dolan said. "We'd have never survived, neither them Injuns nor that mountain, if you'd not come along."

Moses Calhoun shook the young man's hand.

"I reckon I'd be grateful if you didn't mention me, either to the folks in town or to the army folks," he said. "I seem to have made a fair number of enemies out of former friends over the last few days, and the less talk there is about it, the better off I'll be."

"You don't have to worry about us saying anything to the army about it, that's for sure," Hep Chandler said. "As soon as we're able, we're going to buy some clothes and bury these uniforms and get on back to civilian life."

Craig Dolan nodded agreement.

"I've had it with the army," he said. "We signed up to fight Rebels, not to get killed by Injuns."

Calhoun sent them on with two of the ponies, one to carry Chris Dolan and the other to carry the rest of the doe meat and a couple of extra blankets. They'd make the settlement before nightfall, but if they ran into some trouble, Calhoun didn't want them without any provisions. Both soldiers had already resumed possession of their guns, and Calhoun didn't see any need to press the issue now that they were splitting up. He'd had enough dealings with soldiers, though, that he watched his back trail a while to make sure they weren't following him in some foolhardy mission to try to take him prisoner again.

Calhoun and Aka Ne'ai started up the trail with her boys on the last of the three ponies, the sorrel horse and the mule following them. Aka Ne'ai did not mind the walk after so many days of riding.

***

Moses Calhoun always found new strength to make the trek back home. No matter how weary he was on a long hunt, that last climb up the trail never bothered him too much. He'd come up that trail in a blizzard once, and still managed it in a day.

And so it was now. The fresh wounds he'd earned on this latest venture off his mountain still nagged at him, causing him some pain. But Kee Kuttai would look after those as soon as he got to her, and the excitement of seeing his family again filled him with the energy he needed to make the climb.

He'd already decided that Aka Ne'ai and her children would have to stay with him for a few days while he regained his strength. The trek into town and back to deliver Aka Ne'ai to her father would take him two full days, more if there was a fresh snowfall, and he had no desire to leave his family again so soon.

As a man always does on returning home, Moses Calhoun looked through the forest for signs of change. Much of the ground here was still covered in snow, where the canopy of spruce and pine prevented the sun's rays from melting it off. They'd had a good snow, probably much bigger than the one that had covered the western valley and mountains.

The boys, Daniel and Elijah, were out at the firewood pile with the yellow cur dog. They had the ax with them and should have been splitting kindling, Moses knew, but instead they were running and playing a game of tag with the cur dog dancing around them.

When the dog spotted Moses Calhoun far down the trail, he let out a loud bark and some growls and charged forward until he was near enough to see who it was, and then the tail started going like mad and the dog rushed forward, jumping up on Moses and planting one paw right on the wound to his side. He winced and scratched the dog's head, then gently pushed him down. The cur dog went to sniff at the sorrel horse.

Then came the boys, rushing into their father's arms. He kneeled down and caught both boys. They peppered him with questions, to which he gave simple answers.

"Yes, there was quite a bit of snow. Yes, I saw the Indians' camp."

The boys were awkward when Aka Ne'ai's sons climbed down from the pony, and Moses told his sons to help the boys tote the animals into the corral.

"I'll be along in a moment to get the saddle and pack off them," he said.

He took Aka Ne'ai to the cabin where Kee Kuttai was standing at a table cutting vegetables.

"Est tu a la maison?" Kee Kuttai said, turning to see her husband walking through the door of the cabin.

"English," he said with a grin.

"Tu es blesse," she said, putting down her knife and coming toward her husband. "You are hurt," she repeated in English. She had seen the holes in his buckskin shirt and the blood stains on it.

"A bit," Moses said, holding up a hand. "But I'm all right."

He was standing with the door open, and now Aka Ne'ai walked through the door. Kee Kuttai stopped and looked at the woman.

"This is Aka Ne'ai, Eli Simmons' daughter."

"Bonjour," Kee Kuttai said. "Welcome to my home."

But her face was rigid with concern, and she looked back to her husband.

"Entrez vous," she said. "Come in and sit, Aka Ne'ai. Moses, take off that shirt and let me see how bad you are hurt."

He smiled at his wife, whose English came and went depending on her mood.

"Before I take off this shirt, let me go out and tend to the horse and mule," Moses said. "I stay in here much longer and I'll get too comfortable in the warmth."

But stepping back outside, he found it had only taken a few moments inside the cabin to become too comfortable in the warmth. A shiver ran through him as he walked to the corral.

The four young boys stood around outside the rough fence, eying each other and uncertain what to do. At last, little Elijah reached up and tagged the older of Aka Ne'ai's sons and took off running. Even as he watched, the four boys were chasing each other and laughing. Separated by language and the customs of their people, the boys still managed to play and laugh.

As he unsaddled the horse and removed the pack from the mule, Moses Calhoun wondered about the game of chase unfolding in the western valley at the winter camp of the Snake People. He wondered if the soldiers had arrived yet. If not, they surely would soon be there.

He wondered, too, about the young boys he'd sent to the settlement. He'd given them the name of a man down in the little village, Ethan Corder, who Moses Calhoun trusted to help the boys and get them to town. They should have made the settlement by now, and Calhoun had confidence they would be fine, at least getting to the town. If they truly intended to desert from the army, they might be begging for more trouble down the road.

But that was none of his concern.

He stowed the saddle and the bridle in the lean-to barn. He toted the pannier to the front porch of the cabin and set it down in a chair on the porch. The overhang would keep it dry, and he could deal with it later.

Inside, Aka Ne'ai and Kee Kuttai were talking. They stopped when Calhoun entered the cabin, but he'd heard enough of it to know that Aka Ne'ai was relating some of the events of their journey to Calhoun's wife.

"Come close to the fire," Kee Kuttai said, and she stopped what she was doing at the table to tend to her husband's injuries.

She lit a couple of candles to give more light and she examined the wounds. She made tisking sounds as she looked at his side, and she shook her head. But she found a tin with a salve, and she found a couple of bandages.

She did not ask questions or lecture him. She lived in a place where men had to go and do the things they did, and women had to pick up the pieces when it was over. Now she was doing her part, as Moses Calhoun had done his part.

"You sleep," she said, nodding her head toward the loft above them. "When supper is ready, I will wake you."

"Thank you," Moses Calhoun said.

He climbed up into the loft.

Outside, he could hear the children laughing, and the cur dog barked a couple of times.

And then he fell asleep.

The women and the children ate supper while Moses Calhoun slept. Then the women talked late into the evening, well after the sun was down, Aka Ne'ai telling all she could of the journey that brought them from the winter camp to the Calhouns' cabin.

After a couple of days of resting and gaining back his strength, Moses Calhoun again packed his pannier and saddled his horse, and he rode down to the town with Aka Ne'ai and her children, and he took her to her father's cabin in the woods near the town. He did not stay the night, opting instead to return home as soon as possible.

- 26 -

Word spread, as it always did.

Through the winter, trappers and hunters who knew of Moses Calhoun's cabin would come by for a warm meal, a place to spend the night and dry out. And they brought news.

The slaughter at the winter camp had reached terrible proportions.

Some said two hundred Snake People were killed. Many warriors, but women and children, too. Some, who claimed to have gone to the winter camp, said the death toll was even greater. Others said it was less. But it seemed that whatever the actual number, the Snake People's winter camp had been destroyed, and everyone agreed that those who fled and survived the attack of the soldiers would be lucky to survive the winter. Those refugees who escaped the soldiers had no provisions and no protection. They'd fled the winter camp without anything, and when they came back after the soldiers had left, they found all they left behind had been burned by the soldiers. Their teepees, their supplies. What wasn't burned was cut to shreds by the cavalrymen wielding sabers or had been dumped in the river. Stores of flour and salt intended to get the tribe through the winter, all of it dumped into the river.

The soldiers suffered casualties, too, but those numbers were insignificant compared to the Indians killed.

Some said the worst casualties suffered by the soldiers came in the days before the massacre at the winter camp. They said the soldiers were patrolling the valley ahead of the regiment and were ambushed by Snake warriors.

These were the stories that hunters and trappers brought back to Moses Calhoun's cabin over the winter. This was how news spread in the mountains. Moses suspected there was truth in some of it and exaggeration in the rest, but he did not doubt that the Snake People, who had been his friends for many years, had been scattered. He did not doubt that their tribe would never recover. Likely, the survivors would drift toward other tribes or go to one of the government reservations.

In late-spring, when the snow was gone from all but the highest of the peaks, Moses Calhoun took the yellow cur dog with the black mouth, the sorrel horse, and his mule out on a hunt. He intended to be gone only a few days, and he was hunting mostly in the valley below his home. Though earlier in the day he'd seen an elk, too far to shoot, and tracked it higher up a slope.

He had just finished hanging a dressed elk carcass in a tree when the dog began to bark.

By instinct, Calhoun's hand dropped to the hatchet on his belt, and he slipped back in among a couple of small fir trees where he would be hidden. He hissed at the dog, but it stood guard near the tree where he'd hung the elk and continued to growl and bark.

In a moment, a man with a heavy bearskin coat emerged, coming from behind a cluster of trees. He was toting a long, Lancaster rifle. He had a possibles bag, powder horn, and a canteen slung over his shoulder. Wherever he'd come from, he'd come on foot.

Calhoun could not see the man's face for he wore a beaver hat and the collars of his bearskin coat obscured his face. But the man was not wearing gloves, and Moses Calhoun could see that he had all his fingers attached. The cur dog, who gave up the barking in favor of tail wagging, rushed to the man, and he stooped down and scratched the dog. The man was probably a friend and neighbor. And then he called out, and Calhoun recognized the voice.

"Mose Calhoun," Eli Simmons said. "Are you around?"

Calhoun stepped out from behind the trees.

"There you are," Eli said. "What are you doing hiding? You haven't gone scaredy on me?"

Calhoun grinned as he walked out to his old friend.

"Not scared," he said. "Just cautious. I've made some enemies."

Eli Simmons understood. His daughter, of course, had told him of the encounters with Bearclaw Jim and Three Black Feathers.

"Well, I heard the shot and guessed you were probably around close," Eli said. "I stopped by your cabin, and your wife told me you'd gone on a hunt, so I come down into the valley to find you."

"It's a long trek you've made," Calhoun said. "You come all this way on foot?"

Eli nodded.

"I don't get around well much anymore, but I get around a mite better on foot than I do trying to climb in and out of a saddle. And settin' all day in a saddle leaves my legs useless."

Calhoun decided to make his camp there for the night rather than try to take the elk back down to the camp he'd made in the valley. Mostly, he wanted to spare his old friend any more walking for the day.

They made a meal of some meat from the elk and some biscuits Kee Kuttai had sent with her husband, and then they sat by the fire. The night would be cool, but pleasant.

"I've come at my daughter's request," Eli said when the meal was done. "She wants to know if you've heard from her husband."

Moses Calhoun shook his head.

"I'd hoped maybe he made his way to the town without coming to find me first," he said.

"Nope," Eli Simmons said, a strain in his voice.

"Nope. Haven't seen hide nor hair of him. The snow began to melt some weeks ago. No reason a man can't travel now."

Moses nodded.

"I believe that's right," he agreed.

"I reckon we don't have to say it out loud," Eli Simmons said. "Men like us, we know what it means that he hasn't come around."

"I reckon."

The two men spent the next morning together, hunting down in the valley.

A small herd of pronghorns turned up in the valley meadow, and Moses Calhoun left them for Eli Simmons to have a shot. The pronghorns were some distance away, but Moses felt a pang of sympathy for the old hunter when he missed his shot and the herd bounded off, spooked by the rifle.

"I suppose I misjudged the distance a little," Eli Simmons said weakly.

"Easy thing to do," Moses said.

After that, they tied the elk carcass to the mule. Calhoun was disappointed to have just the elk to bring back to his smokehouse, but there was plenty of time for more hunts. The two men hiked the rest of the day back to Corder's cabin where Eli Simmons spent the night before making the trip back to town where he would have to share the disappointing, but not unexpected, news with his daughter.

When Eli Simmons left, Moses Calhoun and his wife, Kee Kuttai, sat a long time in the chairs on the porch of the cabin. The late afternoon air was cool, but the day had been warm enough that they knew summer would be on them soon.

A wistful sort of feeling had come over Moses when he saw his old friend miss a shot that just a few years ago he'd have made nine out of ten times.

"What's troubling you, Moses?" Kee Kuttai asked.

Moses shook his head and frowned. He wasn't sure he could put into words what he was thinking.

"I reckon I'm thinking about life, and death," Calhoun said. "Thinking about that woman Aka Ne'ai, and those two boys of hers."

"You don't think her husband will turn up?" Kee Kuttai asked.

Calhoun shook his head.

"Doesn't seem likely. All those years ago, I saved that boy so that he could grow up to get hisself killed by soldiers."

Kee Kuttai pursed her lips.

"They should have left the winter camp when you told them what was coming," she said. "All of them. The entire tribe."

Moses Calhoun considered that for a moment. He'd had the same thought himself several times over the winter, but he felt he understood why they did not.

"A man's pride will only let him run so many times," Moses Calhoun said. "A man gets to a point where living is no better than dying if he can't stand himself. I reckon they knew what was coming, and I reckon they weighed it out and decided they'd done enough running."

Kee Kuttai made a scoffing noise.

"La vanite," Kee Kuttai said.

"Ha," Moses said, making his own scoffing noise. "It's more than vanity. It's who you are as a man. Are you a man who keeps getting pushed, or are you a man who pushes back? It's what you think of yourself."

"C'est la vie," Kee Kuttai said. "But it still seems better to live your life than give it to the white soldiers."

Moses sighed heavily.

A couple of squirrels that had come down from the safety of the trees scampered quickly back up as the cur dog came charging toward them. The boys, Daniel and Elijah, followed behind the dog, throwing rocks up at the squirrels.

"You have to skin whatever you kill," Moses Calhoun shouted to them with a grin. "And we'll have it for breakfast in the morning."

At the risk of adding to their chores, the boys gave up their rock throwing.

Out through the forest, everything glowed golden green in the spring evening. The sun was going down on the far side of the mountain. The breeze was gentle and cool, and it smelled of earth and pine, a clean scent that spoke of fresh beginnings.

This mountain was not so different from the mountains Moses Calhoun knew as a boy coming up in North Carolina, but he'd come a long way to find it. Adventure brought him out here, the thrill of seeing something other people hadn't seen. A desire to live life on his own terms without a crowd of people to interfere had also driven him. Wasn't that also pride, of a sort?

He thought of an old woman he'd known back in

North Carolina. An old widow, maybe, or maybe just an old maid. He never knew for sure. She was ancient from the time Moses was a little boy, and whatever her past might have been the children could only speculate. Cantankerous and mean so that the children avoided her cabin if they could, but now Moses figured she was just lonely. Solitude, he'd discovered, was better if you had someone to share it with.

"What would you and the children do if something happened to me?" Calhoun asked her.

"We would get along," Kee Kuttai said. "But I would be lonely without you."

Even in the remote wilderness, the troubles of the world had a way of finding a man's doorstep. Moses Calhoun hoped they would get lost before they came back around his way.

THE END

ABOUT THE AUTHOR

Robert Peecher is the author of more than a score of Western novels. He is former journalist who spent 20 years working as a reporter and editor for daily and weekly newspapers in Georgia.

Together with his wife Jean, he's raised three fine boys and a mess of dogs. An avid outdoorsman who enjoys hiking trails and paddling rivers, Peecher's novels are inspired by a combination of his outdoor adventures, his fascination with American history, and his love of the one truly American genre of novel: The Western.

For more information and to keep up with his latest releases, we would encourage you to visit his website (mooncalfpress.com) and sign up for his twice-monthly e-newsletter.

OTHER NOVELS BY ROBERT PEECHER

THE LODERO WESTERNS: Two six-shooters and a black stallion. When Lodero makes a graveside vow to track down the mystery of his father's disappearance, it sends Lodero and Juan Carlos Baca on an epic quest through the American Southwest. Don't miss this great 4-book series!

THE TWO RIVERS STATION WESTERNS: Jack Bell refused to take the oath from the Yankees at Bennett Place. Instead, he stole a Union cavalry horse and started west toward a new life in Texas. There he built a town and raised a family, but he'll have to protect his way of life behind a Henry rifle and a Yankee Badge.

ANIMAS FORKS: Animas Forks, Colorado, is the largest city in west of the Mississippi (at 14,000 feet). The town has everything you could want in a Frontier Boomtown: cutthroats, ne'er-do-wells, whores, backshooters, drunks, thieves, and murderers. Come on home to Animas Forks in this fun, character-driven series.

TRULOCK'S POSSE: When the Garver gang guns down the town marshal, Deputy Jase Trulock must form a posse to chase down the Garvers before they reach the outlaw town of Profanity.

FIND THESE AND OTHER NOVELS BY
ROBERT PEECHER AT AMAZON.COM

Made in United States
Orlando, FL
24 January 2025

57794633R00157